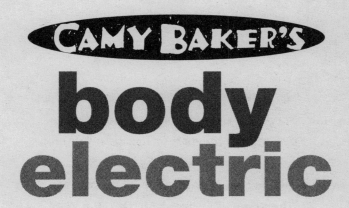

Camy Baker's

body electric

Other books you will enjoy

Libby on Wednesday by Zilpha Keatley Snyder
The Egypt Game by Zilpha Keatley Snyder
The Castle in the Attic by Elizabeth Winthrop
Anastasia Krupnik by Lois Lowry
Wanted . . . Mud Blossom by Betsy Byars
The Summer I Shrank My Grandmother
by Elvira Woodruff
Boys Against Girls by Phyllis Reynolds Naylor

body electric

30 cool rules for a brand-new you

A SKYLARK BOOK

New York • Toronto • London • Sydney • Auckland

RL 5.0, 009–012

CAMY BAKER'S BODY ELECTRIC

A Bantam Skylark Book / February 1999

Skylark Books is a registered trademark of Bantam Books, a division of Random House, Inc. Registered in U.S. Patent and Trademark Office and elsewhere.

A book by Memphis & Melrose Publishing Co.
All rights reserved.
Copyright © 1999 by Memphis & Melrose Publishing Co.
Cover art © 1999 by Bard Martin.

ISBN 0-553-48658-6

Published simultaneously in the United States and Canada.

Bantam Books are published by Bantam Books, a division of Random House, Inc. Its trademark, consisting of the words "Bantam Books" and the portrayal of a rooster, is Registered in U.S. Patent and Trademark Office and in other countries. Marca Registrada. Bantam Books, 1540 Broadway, New York, New York 10036.

PRINTED IN THE UNITED STATES OF AMERICA

OPM   0   9   8   7   6   5   4   3   2   1

a note from camy baker

hey, girls!

My name is Camy Baker, and I'm morphing my way through puberty.

I have a lot of friends, from Beverly Hills, California, to Peoria, Illinois. And they're all morphing too.

Chances are, if you're reading this book, you're going through the same thing.

So what the heck does *morphing your way through puberty* mean?

First of all, let me explain puberty.

For boys, puberty is the time when they start growing into men. They get taller and hairy—kind of like apes! J.k. (Just kidding.)

For girls, it's the time when we develop

1

breasts, get lots of body hair ourselves, and then—bang!—we get our periods.

If you're like me, you're probably wondering why we have to go through this puberty thing at all.

I know, I know. We have to go through puberty so our bodies can become adult bodies. But it sure seems like it would be a lot easier staying a kid. Am I right?

I presented this theory to my mom. I told her I decided it would be easier *not* to go through puberty.

My mom said, "I'd love it if you stayed a little girl forever. But don't you want to grow up? To become an adult?"

That I had to think about. In fact, the question made my life flash before my eyes.

There I was, this adorable little baby bundled in a white blanket, fresh from the hospital a few days after my birth.

Of course I don't remember this moment. But my older sister, Sara, was seven at the time and remembers it clearly. She tells me about it often, so it really feels like I can remember it myself!

Flash forward five years. I'm older, smarter—

and I can walk on my own. I'm in kinder-garten, and I remember jumping rope with my friends in Philadelphia. I'm singing my little heart out, using all the big words I've been learning in class.

I like not being a baby 'cause no one has to carry me around in a white blanket. Plus I can do some mean jumping! ☺

Suddenly a few years pass and I'm in the fifth grade at Beverly Hills Elementary. I look down on kindergartners. Not that I'm mean to them or anything! But I'm a lot taller and stronger and smarter than they are. They're adorable, I must admit, but I'm much happier being a fifth-grader!

Now here I am—in sixth grade at Peoria Middle School. And I am slowly (and I mean *slowly*) developing breasts. Soon I'm going to have my period. Then one day, if I choose, I will have a husband. And I may even one day have a baby.

Pondering my past and imagining my future, I thought about my mom's question: "But don't you want to grow up? To become an adult?"

To be honest, yeah—I guess I *do* want to grow up. In fact, I have no choice!

But if you're like me, you're probably wondering why puberty is so difficult!

If you want to know the truth, puberty can be difficult because everything about us is changing.

One big change we're going through is in the way we think. You might not feel it, but your mind is getting sharper and smarter. It's a very gradual change. You're learning to think in new, deep ways.

But the biggest change, of course, is with our bodies. *That's* what morphing your way through puberty means—the changes your body is going through.

"What's *happening* to me?"

Have you ever asked yourself that? Has your body started to change? Mine sure has.

I personally have been doing so much morphing lately, I feel like one of those kids in the *Animorphs* books. Today Camy's a squirrel. Tomorrow Camy will be a horse! ☺

Just the other day I was checking myself out in the mirror. "I wish I could look in the mirror and be happy and proud of this body of mine," I thought.

I mean, I think I have the smallest chest in

my class. And my legs are getting long and skinny. And my arms are long and gawky.

I tried to forget that a few days earlier a boy called me Spider.

I tried to forget that my friend Jackie has just graduated to her next bra size—when I'm not wearing *anything*!

I tried to forget that every day when I stare into the mirror, it's like I'm seeing a stranger. And like meeting a true stranger, it can be kind of scary.

I decided that instead of being dissatisfied with my new body, though, I was going to try to understand and appreciate it. And I hope what I've learned will help you feel better about your changing body too.

'Cause even though we're going through some major changes right now, there's nothing to be afraid of. After all, once the change is complete, there's going to be a brand-new you!

Just think of a caterpillar. You think a caterpillar is afraid of going through change? Hardly! Once a caterpillar goes through its change, it becomes a beautiful butterfly!

So don't despair. Puberty might be hard, puberty might be confusing, and puberty might be a little scary. But it's a perfectly normal part of growing up. Millions of girls are going through it too. And I promise we'll get through this big change together!

Before I get to the first cool rule, I think it's important to let you know now that this book is not going to cover *every* important topic about puberty. You know, things like which kind of tampon to buy and how to use it.

There are a lot of other wonderful books out there about puberty. My book should be used in addition to them.

And if anything in this book differs from information you've learned at school, in other books, or through your parents, please discuss those differences with your parents or an adult you trust.

Okay, my friend. It's time to take you into this big, bright new world of puberty. So don your butterfly wings and let's fly into the unknown!

part
1 one

accept your body exactly the way it is

this is a rule that is (like most rules, if you think about it) easier said than done. What this means is that it's nice and easy to say, "Okay, I know I have to accept my body exactly the way it is."

But it's actually kind of difficult to accept your body exactly the way it is.

Here are a few reasons why:

You might be frustrated with your body. After all, it's changing *all the time*. "Stop, already!," you say to yourself. "Let me get used to you before you change again!" But of course your body does change again. And again. And again. (And it's gonna keep changing for many years to come!)

9

You might be afraid of your body. After all, it's doing some pretty freaky things! It's kind of hard to accept something that seems strange to you.

You might be impatient with your body. "Hurry up, already!" you think. "I'm dying to see if I'll be like Cindy Crawford, Whitney Houston . . ." or, with a chill, you wonder, "What if I end up looking so strange, I have to travel with the circus?!"

I admit it. We're going to be faced with a lot of challenges when it comes to accepting our bodies.

I've learned that facing a challenge is like taking a test. Sure, taking a test isn't exactly fun. But if you prepare yourself and face the challenge, you become a more confident person once the test is over.

If you still find yourself thinking, "It's too hard. There's so much going on with my body right now, I just can't deal with it, much less accept it," think about this:

Your friends are changing too. And you accept them exactly as they are, don't you?

So why accept your friends exactly the way they are, but not accept yourself that way too?

I mean, friends are important. But the truth is, no one is as important to you as *you*.

If you can't accept your body exactly the way it is, you might become overly concerned with how you look.

This might make you feel insecure about the way you look. And if you always feel insecure, it's going to be hard to be happy with yourself.

Needless to say, when I realized that my happiness depended on my being able to accept myself exactly the way I am, I realized the importance of this rule.

The fact is, we're going to keep morphing until we're about eighteen years old. That means what we're seeing in the mirror now isn't going to be what we end up with.

But we can't wait until we're finished growing, *then* decide to accept our bodies. We have to accept our bodies *now*. Otherwise we're going to be basket cases by the time we finally *do* stop growing!

So if you can accept your body now, while it's going through all these changes, it's going to be totally easy to accept your body when the brand-new you finally emerges!

How cool is that?! ☺

realize you're more than a reflection

this is a true story.

I have a friend named Katy. We go to school together at Peoria Middle School. Katy and I aren't best friends, but we are very close and have a lot of the same classes. In between classes, we occasionally find ourselves in the girls' bathroom together.

I don't wear makeup, so I'm usually washing my hands or fixing my hair. Katy wears makeup, though, so she's usually applying a fresh coat of paint.

One day while washing my hands, I looked up and noticed that Katy was staring at herself in the mirror. For, like, a long time. She was totally motionless—like someone had put her on "pause" or something. It also looked like she was about to cry.

"You okay, Katy?" I asked, kind of concerned.

"I'm hideous."

"You look like you always do," I said.

"You're saying I'm *always* hideous," she snapped.

I didn't *mean* to say she looked hideous every day. I meant to say she didn't look different from any other day. "No, no," I said quickly. "I mean—you look fine."

"Oh, I look *fine*," she shot back. "So you're saying I'm not *beautiful*!"

Suddenly I'm thinking, "She's gone from saying she's hideous to wanting to hear she's beautiful! *Hello,* can we say 'irritating'?!"

"Whatever, Katy," I said, gathering up my books.

"You're a jerk!" she screamed, and stormed past me in a fit of tears.

If you've experienced an episode similar to this, welcome to the world of puberty! And if you've never experienced anything like this, trust me—you will!

Katy's reaction was pretty normal for a girl

going through puberty. After all, she's changing so much, she feels very vulnerable. We've all felt like this at one time or another.

And when we feel vulnerable, for some reason, we tend to convince ourselves we're hideous while also wanting to be told we're beautiful.

Like Katy. She didn't look any different than she did on other days. And I see her enough to know there was absolutely no difference. But she was obviously not feeling great that day, so in her mind she looked hideous.

It's a funny thing about us girls. We tend to have an emotional relationship with the mirror. This means that what we see in the mirror is usually a reflection of how we *feel*, not how we look.

Trust me, there will be days when you look at yourself in the mirror and like what you see. There will also be days when you look in the mirror and *don't* like what you see. This doesn't mean you've suddenly gotten ugly! It just means you're feeling vulnerable.

Instead of being mean to yourself (or others!!!), try to remember this rule: You're more than a reflection.

What this means is that the person staring

back at you in the mirror is not *you*. The real you is the person staring *into* the mirror. The real you has feelings, dreams, and goals—and has a body and a heart.

The girl staring back at you? She's just a reflection of what you think you look like. And on the days when you don't like what you're seeing, it just means you aren't feeling great about yourself.

So basically how you see yourself in the mirror reflects how you're feeling at the moment. Nothing more. Rather than spend time worrying about how you look, maybe you should spend time wondering why you don't feel great.

Maybe you're just having a bad day. Maybe you're not accepting yourself. Whatever it is, try to find out more about your true feelings.

But if you're still having difficulty looking into a mirror and feeling good about what you see, you definitely need to follow the next rule:

limit your time in front of the mirror

pretend you wake up one morning and discover that every single mirror in the world has disappeared.

How would you feel?

Probably a little bummed out. You're so used to looking in mirrors that you might think they're really important.

But after a while you'd get used to a world without mirrors, wouldn't you? After all, if the mirrors weren't there, you wouldn't be able to use them!

Before long you might even start *liking* the fact that there were no mirrors. 'Cause you wouldn't have to worry so much about how you look. You wouldn't have to constantly check yourself in the mirror. You'd just have to *trust* that you look all right.

Do you realize that boys pretty much live in a world without mirrors? Not that boys don't check themselves out in mirrors. They occasionally do.

Most boys I know, though, spend a lot less time in front of mirrors than girls. If you don't believe me, go into the boys' bathroom (which I accidentally did the other day, and was *I* embarrassed!). You won't see a flock of guys fighting for the mirror like you'll find in the girls' bathroom.

Since guys don't spend very much time in front of the mirror, they tend to think they're better looking than they really are. Have you ever noticed that? I have. At first I found it irritating, but now I kind of like it. I mean, we should all feel confident about the way we look. I really think boys are better at feeling confident about their looks because they don't use mirrors as much as we do.

A big reason girls spend so much time in

front of the mirror is that there's a lot of pressure on us to look a certain way. (I totally get into this issue later in the book!)

Another reason is because some girls wear makeup and have complicated hairstyles. Makeup and hairstyles continually need touching up. Obviously, you need the help of a mirror for touch-ups!

Now, I'm not saying you can't wear makeup, or have complicated hairdos, or ever look in the mirror again!

I *am* saying the more you look at something, the harder it's going to be to appreciate it. Let me explain.

I check myself in a mirror at least four times a day. Once before school, once during school, once when I get home (to see if my breasts have grown!!!), and once more when I brush my teeth before bed.

That means in one year I will have seen myself in the mirror 1,460 times. And that's if I check myself out only four times a day!

Now let's pretend you're forced to look at a picture of you favorite actor 1,460 times.

The first 500 times you might love looking at him.

18

The next 500 times you might enjoy looking at him—but you know what he looks like and he's kind of getting on your nerves.

After the next 500 times all you see is his big, fake smile and pimply little chin. You tear the photo off the wall, wad it up into a ball, and say to yourself, "If I ever see his face again I'm going to hurl!"

What happens when you look at something too much? You get bored with it—or sick of it! Not only that, but you'll probably start finding all kinds of things wrong with it.

So if you stare at yourself in the mirror way too much, it's totally plausible you might find yourself getting supercritical of the way you look.

Want to know what happens when you get supercritical of yourself? I hope so, 'cause it's the next rule!

reprogram your thoughts

I don't want to scare you. But there's a girl in your life and she's out to get you. You better watch out, because this girl can be vicious.

Oh, sometimes she's okay. Like anyone, she has her good days.

It's the bad days you need to look out for. 'Cause this girl can be spiteful. She can say some truly awful things to you. "Your face is so ugly, you make me sick." Or "Why can't you have blond hair instead of that frizzy red mess?" Or "If your lips were any thinner, you wouldn't even have a mouth!"

When this girl is having a bad day, she calls

you mean names, makes fun of the way you look, and tries to convince you that you're ugly.

If you don't know a girl like this, dig deeper and I think you'll find her.

Because she's *you*.

I never realized I had this evil girl inside me until one day—a really bad day for me—I said to myself out loud: "You are the most disgusting thing I have ever seen."

"What did I just say?!" I immediately thought. "Where did *that* come from?"

To tell you the truth, I'm glad I said it. Because ever since I said that truly awful thing, I realized I said those kinds of things all the time without even knowing it. I never said them out loud. I said them in my head.

My sister, Sara, is always reminding me to pay close attention to the thoughts I have about myself. She said these thoughts are very, very important. But until I *said* that rude comment to myself, I didn't realize I was *thinking* mean thoughts about myself. So you, too, might be thinking mean thoughts about yourself without even realizing it.

I totally agree with Sara. Our thoughts

about ourselves are very, very important. In fact, they form the basis of how we *feel* about ourselves.

And if you think mean thoughts about yourself, you're not accepting yourself exactly the way you are. Which means, of course, you're breaking rule number one!

So if you think mean thoughts about yourself (and it will take some practice to figure out if you do), it's time to quit, girl! You need to do what I did and pretend you're a computer. It's time to be reprogrammed!

Reprogramming yourself is very simple. The first step to ending those mean thoughts is to recognize them when you think them.

They'll often pop into your head when you're looking in the mirror.

For instance, you look in the mirror and think, "I wish I wasn't so ugly," or any other supercritical thought. You were just mean to yourself.

Or you look into the mirror and wish you looked like someone else. Or you think "I wish I had blond hair." You were just mean to yourself. Because what you just said was, "Blond hair is better, and my hair is just not good enough."

I've learned that it takes a lot of practice to figure out when you're being mean to yourself. You just have to pay attention to your thoughts—particularly when you're looking in the mirror.

Once you recognize that you're being mean to yourself, you need to immediately turn the negative thought into a happy thought.

You do this by focusing on the things you *like* about yourself.

Instead of saying, "I wish I wasn't so ugly," you can say, "I really love that my skin is so smooth and beautiful." Or "I love that my hair is very thick. And the color is *FIERCE*!" Or "My eyes are gor-G-ous!" Say whatever works for you.

I think you'll find you have some really wonderful qualities. You just need to focus on your strengths, not your weaknesses!

Maybe you have a hard time complimenting yourself because you're afraid that will mean you're stuck-up. But which is worse: being stuck-up, or emotionally beating yourself up?

Think about it!

I'm not saying you have to run around school and brag about yourself. But there is absolutely nothing wrong with admitting that you have great features.

But there is *definitely* something wrong with being mean to yourself.

Reprogramming your thoughts basically means this: Work on being nice to yourself, rather than being mean to yourself.

Just remember: The thoughts you have today are the thoughts you'll carry with you into tomorrow. And if you can start thinking happy thoughts about yourself now, you're going to have a *very* wonderful future! ☺

what's in a name?

Okay, now it's time to explain what the title of this book means.

As you probably know, electricity is a form of energy that powers the really important things in our lives: our blow dryers, our curling irons, our stereos, and our televisions. Oh yeah— our computers and lights, too.

I decided to call this book *Body Electric* because I like the idea that my body is filled with electricity. (My dad works for the electric company, so I know a lot about electricity!)

One day my dad took me on a trip to visit a power plant, where all the electricity is made. He said, and I will never forget, "There is a lot of power in those plants, Camy. And we have to keep them in tip-top shape. Otherwise we wouldn't have any power."

At that moment I began to think there was electricity running through my body. And I decided from that day forward to keep my body in tip-top shape.

My body isn't really filled with electricity, of course. Otherwise I might be a superhero instead of a sixth-grader!

But my body *is* filled with energy. And so is yours.

And since our bodies are filled with energy, that means they're filled with power.

We have the ability to do some pretty amazing things with all this power running through us.

We have the power to be good people. We have the power to love people. We have the power to make the world a better place.

But since we're going through puberty, it can be difficult to remember we have power. Why? Well, because our bodies are changing so much, we usually get caught up with how we look instead.

That's why you hear or ask questions like these: "Does my butt look fat?" "Am I too skinny?"

"Is my nose too big?" "Am I gross?" "Am I pretty?" "I wish I was taller!" "I wish I had breasts!"

But have you ever noticed? No one ever asks questions like these: "Do my lungs look okay?" "Is my heart too big?" "Is my brain pretty?"

If someone asked you those kinds of questions, you'd probably run away as fast as your feet could carry you!

It's natural to spend more time worrying about how we look than working on keeping our bodies in tip-top shape. After all, you see the outside of your body. You don't see what's going on inside.

But if you want to know the truth, taking care of the inside of your body is a great way to feel your best. And when you feel your best, you're going to have the power it takes to be confident enough to accept yourself exactly the way you are.

So if you want more help accepting *you* (and who doesn't?!), you're going to have to keep your body running in tip-top shape. And what we put *into* our bodies is the most important part of keeping them healthy.

Are your butterfly wings still on? Good! Let's fly through the next few rules!

water—you need water!

did you know you could not live more than a few days if your body didn't get any water?

When my mom told me that, I tripped out! I never realized how important water was to our bodies!

I was even more surprised to discover in my research that our bodies are made up of 70% water.

Isn't that weird?! You can't see it. And you can't hear it jiggling around. But we're mostly water!!!

If you're like my friends or me, though, drinking water isn't something you normally think about.

I mean, when you're thirsty you might stop at a drinking fountain and get a few slurps before class. But when you eat breakfast, lunch, or dinner, water isn't something you normally include with your meals. Am I right? Usually you'll grab a soda or milk or something. And that's okay.

You don't necessarily have to drink water to get water. Milk has lots of water in it.

Fruits and vegetables have lots of water in them. In fact, fruits and vegetables are mostly water—just like your body.

So you get a lot of the water you need from the foods you eat, especially natural foods.

If you don't like to eat a lot of fruits and vegetables, though, the other way to get water into your body is to drink it: from bottles, the fountain at school, or the tap at home.

Your body needs *tons* of water. If you don't get enough water, you might get dehydrated.

One sign of being dehydrated is feeling tired. Also, if your lips become really chapped, it might mean your body isn't getting enough water.

Dry skin is another sign your body needs water. Most girls I know use lotion when their skin gets dry. That's fine. But did you realize it's better to tackle the problem from the inside? You guessed it. By drinking more water, you can keep your skin healthier from the inside out.

So drink more water!

I actually know a few girls who are *afraid* to drink water.

Have you ever heard a friend say "God, I'm retaining water" as a way of explaining why she's feeling bloated? And she avoids water so she won't retain any more?

Wrong!

Drinking water won't make you retain water. Did you know that? In fact, drinking water helps keep the inside of your body clean. You're less likely to retain water when you drink water!

Did you know that sodas, on the other hand, *can* make you retain water. In fact, anything unnatural that you put into your body can make you retain water.

The reason is simple. While there's a lot of water in soda, there are also a lot of chemicals (particularly in diet soda).

Your body doesn't know what the heck

these chemicals are. It totally wants to get rid of them.

So your body takes water from where it could be better used and puts it into your bloodstream to get rid of the chemicals. That means that drinking or eating anything with a lot of unnatural chemicals in them can lead to dehydration, chapped lips, and dry skin.

Now, I'm not saying you have to give up soda. I *am* saying that your body needs water a lot more than it needs soda—or anything else with unnatural chemicals in it.

So how much water do you need? Considering your body is 70% water, you probably need a lot more of it than you think!

There's really no way you can drink too much water. Either your stomach is not going to be able to hold it, or you'll just pee the water right out!

So when considering how much water you should drink, remember this: Too much water is always better than not enough!

6

fuel your body

i mentioned in the beginning of the book that a boy recently called me a spider.

His comment was very rude and mean, and I gave him a piece of my mind. "Who do you think you are, judging me?" I said. "I'll have you know that I am in the process of growing and changing. I may be a little skinny now, but it doesn't mean I won't be Cindy Crawford later!"

It felt good telling him exactly what I thought about his rude comment.

But what did I do when I went home? I opened up the cupboards and refrigerator and started eating everything in sight!

My mom came into the kitchen. I guess I

looked strange stuffing snacks into my mouth while holding the refrigerator door open with my foot. (I did this so I could quickly reach for the milk when I was done eating!)

"Camy! What are you doing?" my mom yelled, alarmed.

"I don't know," I said. My mouth was so full, though, it came out more like "I doe doe."

Obviously my mom knew something was wrong. She took the Little Debbies out of my hands and wiped my mouth off with a paper towel. Then she sat me down for a long talk.

I told my mom about the boy calling me a spider. I also told her I was really upset because I was superskinny, had no breasts, and had long arms and gawky legs.

"Just because you're that way now, Camy, doesn't mean that's the way you'll always be," my mom told me.

"That's what *I* told him," I complained.

"So why are you eating like there's no tomorrow?"

I knew the answer. I realized I'd let some kid's rude comment affect the way I was feeling about myself. I really hate it when that happens. "I guess I was trying to speed things up a bit. I figured if I ate a lot, I'd grow more round or something. Then I wouldn't look like a spider anymore."

"So you turned to food to make yourself feel better?"

I sighed. "Yeah. I guess I did."

My mom proceeded to give me the whole food lecture. I'll spare you the nuts and bolts, but it's important I tell you the main points of our discussion.

She was really concerned that if I started getting all weird about food now and began turning to it when I felt bad about myself, I'd always have a weird relationship with food.

Don't laugh. There *is* such a thing as having a *relationship* with food.

Some girls like me turn to food to help solve our problems. It's like we think of food as a friend. If we're having a bad day, or feel upset, or are frustrated with our bodies, we turn to food to make us feel better.

I know some girls who think of food as an *enemy*. They think they need to lose weight, so they avoid food as much as possible.

My mom helped me see that food isn't a friend. And food *isn't* an enemy.

Food is the fuel your body needs to run. Other than water, food is the most important thing we can give our bodies!

As our bodies are morphing through puberty, we need food more than ever! We're growing and growing and growing. Our bodies need tons of fuel so we can reach our proper height and weight.

And your body uses food for its fuel.

When I say you need tons of fuel, I don't mean you should eat everything in sight! It's very important to eat *just* the right amount of food.

"So how do I know if I'm eating *just* the right amount of food?" you might be asking yourself.

I'm so glad you asked!

7

listen to your body

There you are, sitting in class, trying to focus on an important exam. For some reason you're finding it really hard to concentrate. Suddenly your stomach growls. It's so loud that kids look up from their test!

What happened is, your body spoke. And what did it tell you? Girl, you are *hungry*!

The great thing about our bodies is that they're very smart. Your body knows how much food it needs. All you have to do is listen to it.

What that means is, you have to pay attention to the way your body feels. For instance, if you're really hungry, you'll feel hunger pains and your stomach will growl. Your body is telling you it needs food.

But if you eat too much food, your body will tell you it's had enough.

One way you know you've had enough food is when your stomach feels stuffed. You know the feeling. You think, "If I eat one more piece of Aunt Nancy's apple pie, I'm going to hurl!" (By the way, barfing is one way your body lets you know it's had too much food!)

All you have to do is listen to your body. Eat when you feel hungry. Stop eating when you're full. How simple is that?

So what happens if you don't eat enough food or you eat too much? Actually, very similar things happen. Believe me, I've felt them both!

If I'm having a crazy day, sometimes I forget to eat. And sometimes I can be so busy that I even ignore my hunger pains.

But when I ignore my hunger pains for too long, I totally get supertired.

You know how a car will stop when it runs out of gas? Well, that's just what happens to me when I don't fuel my body.

The strange thing is, when I eat too much I feel the same way!

Last Thanksgiving I stuffed myself to maximum overload—and felt very tired afterward.

Sara tells me that when you eat too much, your body has to work overtime to digest everything.

And believe it or not, digesting food takes up a lot of energy. And when your body has to digest turkey, gravy, biscuits, cranberry sauce, and pecan pie—well, it doesn't have much energy left to do anything else!

Have you ever taken a nap or become a couch potato and vegged out in front of the TV after Thanksgiving dinner? Well, now you know why!

There will be times when you'll eat too much. That's totally okay. But try not to make a habit of eating when you're not hungry. And try not to make a habit of eating so much that you feel *way* too full.

Because if you do that on a regular basis, chances are you're eating as a way to make yourself feel better about something else.

Here's what I do when I'm having a difficult day and start to turn to food to make me feel better. Before eating, I tell myself that in five minutes I'll snack if I want to. But first I'm going to write in my journal and try to figure out what I'm feeling right then.

You know what happens when I do this? I get so absorbed in working out my problems, I totally forget about eating until I really become hungry.

Trust me. It's better to turn to your journal when you're feeling funky than to food.

There's one final reason why it's important to listen to your body when it comes to food.

As I mentioned earlier, it's better to get too much water than not enough.

Well, as Sara explained to me, food is different. You can't get rid of excess food as easily as excess water. All the food you eat has to go through your stomach and your intestines (gross!), where the nutrients are absorbed.

It's a long and involved process to digest food, and it uses up a lot of your body's energy.

That's why it's really important to listen to your body when it comes to food. It's better to eat just enough—not too little and not too much!

stop pinching yourself

In the first grade, I used to pinch boys who really ticked me off. Usually I got in a lot of trouble for doing it. One time I nearly lost a finger when a boy tried to bite it off in retaliation!

Obviously, pinching and biting are both *very* mean things to do.

Now, I haven't seen any girls bite themselves. But I have *definitely* seen girls pinch themselves.

They usually do it when they think no one else is looking. They'll be standing there, talking to a friend. You'll see a hand go up to the waist. That would be fine if the girl was just resting her hand on her waist.

40

But then you see the girl's fingers digging into her flesh.

"Why is she pinching herself?" you're probably asking? Simple. She's checking to see how much fat she's got!

If the girls at your school are anything like the girls at mine, they talk about fat as if it's evil and needs to be avoided at all costs.

Wrong!

Remember, your body is very smart. It puts fat where fat needs to be.

Fat is an important part of our bodies, or obviously it wouldn't be there!!! Instead of living in terror of fat, it's really important to understand why the fat is there to begin with!

Your body needs fat for a lot of reasons. For one, your body converts fat into energy. That means your body uses fat when it needs fuel and isn't getting it from food.

Fat also warms your body. Fat protects the organs in your body. Fat helps you absorb important vitamins like A, D, E, and K, which you get from certain foods. Fat is also what makes up our breasts. Our boobs are mostly fat.

If you want to know the truth, pinching yourself to see how much fat you've got is pointless. Just because you can pinch some fat doesn't mean you *are* fat!

Besides, a lot of girls pinch themselves and think they're pinching fat. But really what they're pinching is skin.

To prove this point, here's an exercise to try. Put your right hand up to your ear. With your left hand, pinch the very tip of your elbow. You can't pinch much of anything.

Now extend your right arm all the way out. Now with your left hand, grab as much stuff as you can in the same spot—the very, very tip of your elbow.

You can pinch an inch, right? I know I can! That's skin! The reason it's there is that your elbows are mobile; they can move. We need a lot of skin on our elbows. Otherwise we wouldn't be able to bend them!

Now I want you to bend your leg back all the way to your butt. (Do this while your sitting in a chair!) Now pinch your knee. You can't pinch anything, right? Now hold your leg out and pinch your knee. You can grab at least half an inch, if not more! Are you fat? I don't *think* so.

You've got skin—all over your body. When

you pinch yourself, a lot of what you're pinching is skin, not fat!

Now, I'm not saying you won't be pinching fat, too. And I'm not saying too much fat is a good thing. When people get really obese (which means they have too much fat on their bodies), it can lead to a lot of health problems.

But how many girls do you know who are worried about being fat because of health problems? I personally don't know a single one!

Weighing yourself is almost as bad an idea as pinching yourself.

Did you realize that as you're going through puberty, you're going to gain about forty-five pounds?

Unless you hear otherwise from a doctor or an adult you trust, why worry about how much you weigh? Or how much fat you have on your body? Remember, you're not going to stop growing until around the age of eighteen.

If you worry too much about fat now, you might do some really unhealthy things to your body to try to make yourself thin.

Some girls I know are so concerned with being too fat, they quit listening to their bodies.

They ignore their hunger and cut back on their food to lose weight.

Sure, by cutting back on food, they might make themselves lose weight.

But they also might make themselves very weak.

This can lead to very serious health problems.

9

go for strength, not thinness

a few months back, I had the wonderful opportunity to go on a vacation to Maui with my very good friend Rachel. We used to be classmates at Beverly Hills Elementary.

The last day of the trip, Rachel and I stopped into a really cool bathing suit shop in the airport, just to kill some time before my flight back home. We noticed this adorable girl—she was probably about nine—who was trying on a flowered one-piece bathing suit.

"How cute!" we whispered to each other.

The bathing suit really did look cute on her, and we expected her to be totally excited.

Instead this girl looked very upset. She kept

45

checking herself from every angle—front, back, side. She held her hand over her stomach and pinched her legs. She looked right at me and asked, "Do I look fat?"

Rachel and I were so shocked, we were speechless! The girl gave us this look, like, "You're no help!" Then she turned back to the mirror and said, "I think I need to go on a diet."

I couldn't believe it! I wanted to grab that little nine-year-old and scream, "Be patient with yourself, for crying out loud! You're nine years away from the end of your growth cycle, so chill out!"

I just stood there and watched as the girl continued to check herself out in the mirror. It was like she was an experienced fashion model, checking every angle for her imperfections.

This episode really bummed me out. What is happening to this world when a nine-year-old girl is worried about being fat? I'm a whole three years older than she is—and it freaks me out when girls *my* age worry about being fat!

Some girls might think, "Well that's fine and good, because you're totally skinny." Just because I'm skinny now doesn't guarantee I'll always be skinny. Besides, I've learned something very important, and I hope you can learn it too.

If you're the kind of girl who diets (you restrict the food you eat to lose weight) you should know you're depriving yourself of something very important—your energy.

And when you don't have energy, you don't have strength.

Have you ever heard of a boy going on a diet? I haven't. You know why? 'Cause boys are encouraged to eat a lot of food so they can get big and strong.

News flash! Our bodies are made up of the same things as boys'!

Of course our bodies are built different from theirs. But why should a boy be strong and not a girl? I say, *Snap!* I might not win an arm-wrestling match with Kenny Styler, an eighth-grade football player who lifts weights, but I wouldn't go down without a fight!

If you want to know the truth, I don't know many girls who wouldn't mind being strong. But for some reason, they think it's more important to be thin.

It all goes back to fat.

Let's pretend you don't have any fat on your

body. If you don't have any fat on your body, your body doesn't have a natural place to get energy when it needs it.

So your body has to get the energy it needs from the food you eat.

But let's say you don't have any fat on your body *and* you don't eat much or that often.

Your body still needs *something* for fuel.

Do you know what your body will do to get fuel?

As a last resort, it will start breaking down your muscles to get the fuel it needs.

This is a very dangerous situation. Your body is starving. It wants food, but you're not giving it food. So your body begins eating your muscles to feed itself.

Girls who reach this level of starvation can die. You know why?

Your heart, one of the most important parts of your body, is a muscle. And when your body starts breaking down your muscles for fuel, your heart becomes weak. If your heart gets too weak, it stops working.

I don't say all this to scare you. I'm telling you this because I don't want you to do something that may hurt your body.

Now, I'm not saying that if you think you are overweight, you really aren't. According to my research, there are plenty of overweight kids out there.

But just because you *think* you need to lose weight doesn't mean you really do. And if you're concerned about your weight, don't restrict the food you eat.

Instead, I strongly suggest you go to a doctor or a nutritionist. If they decide you're overweight and it's going to cause health problems, they won't tell you to stop eating. They'll encourage you to eat natural foods and become more active.

If you can't see a doctor or a nutritionist, I strongly suggest you go to your school nurse.

The nurse will look at a height-and-weight chart to get an idea of how much you should weigh. But it'll only be a rough idea because every body is different.

And that's a very important thing to remember: *Every body is different*. Bodies grow at different rates.

I know this is a confusing issue. And I know you probably have a lot more questions. That's why I suggested that you talk to a doctor, a nutritionist, or a nurse. They'll have the most current information on natural foods and why eating them is important.

In the end, though, I really want you to start *trusting* your body. It's smart and knows what it's doing.

Second of all, I don't want you to do anything to your body when you don't know exactly what you're doing. Don't go on a diet. Instead, eat healthier and more natural foods. If you have questions about nutrition and want to learn how to eat healthier and more natural foods, ask someone! Get help!

But the most important thing to remember is this: Don't worry so much about being fat. Worry instead about feeling good! Can you jog without getting tired? Do you feel alert and happy throughout the day? Do you feel ready to take on the world?

If you do, chances are you feel strong. And although some people might disagree with me, I believe being strong is *way* more important than being thin.

And I hope you agree with me! ☺

keep yourself well groomed

When I was younger, life was so much simpler. I didn't have to think about my body very much. Not to be gross or anything, but I could go days without showering. And who knew? I certainly didn't mind, and no one ever said anything.

But now? Hello!

Can we say "pimples" and "body odor" and "greasy skin" and all those other conditions that puberty seems to breed?

If you want to know the truth, going through puberty can be downright disgusting! Now that we are going through it, though, it's very important to keep ourselves well groomed.

What does it mean to be well groomed? Being well groomed basically means you've done everything you possibly can to make sure the outside of your body is clean. The first step to keeping yourself well groomed, obviously, is to shower or bathe once a day.

When puberty kicked in for me, I started sweating a lot more than I used to. I realized that if I didn't wash the sweat and dirt off my skin and hair, pronto, I'd start smelling a little funky. I take a shower at least once a day; maybe two, depending on how stinky I get.

Showering or bathing once a day also helps keep your skin clean. That's important if you don't want to break out in acne. And who does?

I also started using deodorant to keep my pits smelling fresh throughout the long school day. You should consider using a deodorant, if you don't already.

If you're not sure whether you need to use deodorant, here's something to consider: You live with yourself 24/7, so you might be smelly and not even know it. If people hold their nose when you walk by, try some deodorant!

A word about perfume. If you use it, great.

But remember to use perfume sparingly, maybe two or three spritzes at the most. Just because you like the smell of it doesn't mean everyone else will!

Here's another thing I do now that I never did before. I wash my clothes after wearing them just one time. My mom once griped me out about this, saying, "You can wear your jeans more than once before putting them in the laundry basket."

I reminded her I was currently morphing my way through puberty. And I invited her to smell my clothes as I put them in the hamper.

She stopped complaining.

Not to sound like your parents, but don't forget to brush your teeth! If you don't do it for yourself, do it for people like me—people who think bad breath is one big turnoff!

One last thing to keep clean is your nails. I personally keep my nails fairly short, and I clip, clean, and file them once a week.

In fact, grooming my nails is a wonderful way for me to relax. Just chilling out in front of the TV, devoting a little attention to myself, is very comforting. (When you clip your nails, remember to keep track of where the clippings fly off to! My mom gets really irritated when she finds fingernails on the floor!)

As far as shaving goes—you know, pits, bikini line, and leg hair—fortunately this is a situation I've not had to deal with yet. But if you're starting to get hair, you should really ask your mom, an older sister, or a woman you trust about shaving. (And you may not want to do it. It's your body, so it's your choice.) Shaving can be dangerous. You're dealing with a sharp razor, don't forget. You can cut yourself up pretty badly if you don't know what you're doing! So I strongly encourage you to get some expert advice in this area.

Okay, now that we're talking about keeping our bodies clean, I guess it's time to talk about a way our body keeps *itself* clean!

If you haven't guessed, it's time to talk about your period!

ready or not—here it comes

as you may or may not know, your period is your body's way of cleaning our your reproductive system (the things inside your body that help you make a baby).

It might look and feel weird, but having your period is very natural. It's nothing to be frightened or ashamed of.

That said . . .

Period. Ugh! That one little word freaks me out. I live in fear and anticipation of it.

Chances are, if you haven't gotten your period yet, you're a little frightened and excited about it too.

If you want to know the truth, your period is probably the most complicated part of puberty.

It's complicated physically: Do I use tampons or pads? Will I have PMS? What is PMS? Will I go crazy when I get PMS? How will I know it's PMS?

It's complicated emotionally: What's this stuff coming out of me?! I have to put that thing where?! Help!!!!

It's complicated to think about: Why can I make babies? I'm only twelve years old. I don't want to make babies. Why does my period happen at such a young age? I'm not even an adult yet, for crying out loud!

There are so many complicated things about having your period that I could devote an entire book to the subject! But considering I haven't had my period yet—*and* I have to get through nineteen more rules!—I'm going to have to encourage you to discuss your period with your mom, an older sister, or any woman you trust.

I personally have already asked a million questions about my period. And I pretty much know when I'm going to get it.

For those who are curious, my big day will

be sometime next year. How do I know? My mom told me so. She doesn't work for the Psychic Hotline or anything. You usually get your period around the same time your mom got hers. Ask your mom when she got hers so you'll at least be a little more prepared.

But if you can't ask your mom or don't feel comfortable asking her about it, that's okay. There are plenty of women out there who can help you figure out what to do about your period. They won't be able to tell you when you're going to get it, but they'll be able to tell you a lot of other important things you need to know.

Just remember, there's no reason to go through your period alone. If you feel you can't discuss your period with your mom, ask a female teacher. Or your school nurse (if it's a woman). Or your librarian (if it's a woman). Or an aunt, a grandmother, or a friend's older sister. Don't get all your advice from friends just yet. They're still learning too and might not know all the facts.

Also try to remember that every woman has experienced the fear and excitement that comes with starting her period. And I think you'll find that any woman you approach with questions will be very understanding. She'll know it's important for you to know everything you possibly can about what to expect and what to do.

There are also many good books out there that can help you. While I personally believe it's better to get most of your information from an adult you trust, I also strongly urge you to read about what to expect from your period.

After all, the more you know about your period, the less confused or frightened you'll be!

it's your puberty and you can cry if you want to

Dear Journal:

It's 1:52 P.M. on Sunday afternoon and I'm crying my eyes out. Why? Well, no reason. I'm listening to a sad song, but other than that, there's no reason for the tears.

I think I'm going to turn this into a rule. It's a good thing to cry—even if there's no reason. Sometimes I just feel a buildup of confusing emotions. Tears seem like the best way to get them out.

I'm not sad or depressed or anything. I just feel like crying. It feels good to cry and let it all out. I do it a lot lately. I guess it's the whole puberty thing.

Sometimes when I start crying, it's just for a few seconds. I feel tears on my cheeks, and that's it. Other times, it starts off with a few tears and then I totally start sobbing.

One day Sara heard me and rushed into my room, wondering what was wrong. I told her I just felt like crying. She said she understood. She did it sometimes too.

When I start crying and it turns into major sobbing, I turn up my radio and cry into my pillows.

I like to cry without having to explain to Sara or my parents that nothing is wrong. . . .

CAMY'S NOTE:

That, dear readers, was my very own personal journal entry.

Crying doesn't have to mean you're sad, although you could be. Crying doesn't have to mean you're angry or upset, although you could be feeling that way too.

Crying, especially when you're going through puberty, is something that just seems to happen. It's a totally natural thing.

Not only is it natural, but crying is also good for us.

You know how after it rains, the streets are really clean? Well, after you cry, your feelings have been cleaned out too.

It's like writing in a journal—only without a pen.

relax, it's just your hormones

as I mentioned in the previous rule, you might find yourself crying more now than ever.

You might also feel a bunch of other emotions—like anger, happiness, confusion, and a few other things you've never felt before—all in the span of two minutes!

It's like you're on an emotional roller coaster. One minute you love everything. The next minute you're convinced everyone is out to get you.

One minute you're sure you're destined to be the greatest, most famous actress ever. The next minute you just hope to find the energy to get through drama class.

Are you crazy? Why are you feeling up, then down; up, then down?

Actually, you're not crazy.

You're just reacting to your hormones.

What are hormones?

Well, hormones are natural chemicals released by your body into your blood. Your hormones are the things that tell your body to grow.

Hormones can do some pretty funky things to your feelings. They can also do some pretty funky things to your body.

If you want to see just how powerful your hormones are, let's take a look at what they're doing to my best friend, Jackie.

In the last few months, Jackie has started getting a lot taller and rounder. Her breasts are growing, and she's even got pubic hair (which I can't help noticing when we're changing clothes around each other).

Jackie's started her period, she sweats more, and she's even getting pimples.

All the work of hormones.

As you can tell, going through puberty means your hormones are working overtime! Our hormones are more powerful now than they've ever been before. And our hormones play a huge part in the changes we experience with our feelings and our bodies.

Unfortunately, there's not a lot you can do about your hormones. You can't get them removed. And hormones aren't like a headache— you can't take an aspirin and hope they'll go away!

But if you ever find yourself feeling in a funky mood, just remember that you're not crazy. You're probably just reacting to your very powerful hormones.

There is, however, a great way to take your mind off the hormonal roller coaster. And that leads me to the next rule:

14

get physical

i mentioned in the previous rule that hormones can make you feel funky at times.

And in rule number nine, I mentioned that if you were to go to your family doctor, a nutritionist, or your school nurse because you were concerned about your weight, they'd probably encourage you to become more active.

Well, basically what we're talking about here is exercise. You know, moving your body through some physical activity for at least thirty minutes or so? The thing we do in PE.

But let's face it. PE can be boring sometimes. It's like we're these little robots. Who wants to do something over and over, like jumping jacks or sit-ups? Some kids don't have a problem with this, but I do.

Now don't get me wrong. I know the value of exercise. But I don't like the concept of exercise. Exercise sounds boring.

I think that instead of exercising, we should get physical.

Getting physical is better than exercise because you're choosing a physical activity you enjoy doing. You don't have to jog or lift weights or ride a bike (unless those are things you like to do). You can get physical in any number of ways!

Let me give you a few examples. Hiking, in-line skating, skateboarding, walking, dancing, swimming.

I realize some of these activities cost money. If your parents don't have the money to shell out for in-line skates or a bike, don't despair!

There are plenty of ways to get physical that don't cost a lot of money. Let me tell you how I do it.

Remember how I said in the beginning of the book that I really loved to jump rope? Well, guess what? I *still* jump rope! I saved up ten

dollars and bought a really nice jump rope—
the kind that famous boxers train with!

Jumping rope is one of the absolutely *best*
things you can do for your body. For one thing,
jumping rope works most of your major muscles. For another, it's great workout for your
heart—the most important muscle in your
whole body!

Dancing to your favorite song is another
great (and free!) way to get physical. Pop in a
CD, barricade your bedroom door, and get
busy! Dance like you've never danced before.
No one's watching, so go for it!

Playing sports is another terrific way to get
physical. And sports can help you build a lot of
great skills that will help you later in life.

But some girls think it's not cool to play
sports. "It's unladylike," they might say.

That raises a big question. Are there certain
things a girl can and cannot do? For instance, a
girl can be a cheerleader. But can she be a
sports star?

I hope I can answer that question in the
next rule:

15

stay true to yourself

the other day I was at the grocery store with my mom. We noticed this little girl—probably five—and she was singing this song:

"My name is Lisa and I'm a ballerina. My best friend's Nancy and she's an astronaut. We eat peanut butter 'cause we like it so much. And I got straight A's 'cause I'm so smart!"

As soon as Lisa noticed I was watching her, though, she got totally embarrassed. She stopped singing and hid behind her mother, acting all shy.

It was so cute!

Afterward, for some reason, I couldn't stop thinking about Lisa.

Later that night, writing in my journal, I realized I used to sing little songs like that all that time. "Why don't I sing those little songs anymore?" I wondered. They were so much fun!

Curious about this, I went into the living room, where my mom was doing a crossword puzzle. "Mom, remember that girl Lisa in the grocery store today?"

"Lisa?"

"You know, the little girl who was singing that really cute song."

"Oh, right."

"Well, I used to sing songs like that, right?"

"All the time. They were just as cute," my mom said.

"Do you remember when I stopped?"

My mom put down her puzzle and started thinking. "Come to think of it, I don't remember hearing any songs out of you after your tenth birthday. I guess that would have been the fourth grade."

"Why do you think I stopped?" I asked.

"I suppose you stopped for the same reason little Lisa did—she became embarrassed when she realized someone was listening."

"Thanks," I said, and went back into my room.

I'm not sure if my mom really could remember when I stopped singing songs. Maybe she was just humoring me. But I *did* kind of remember fourth grade being just about the time.

"Why am I letting this bother me?" I wondered. I really had no idea. But for some reason, it started me thinking about this girl I used to know.

It was the fourth grade at Beverly Hills Elementary. This girl I used to know was a total tomboy. She loved to spit loogies, and she chewed gum, and she could climb trees faster than a squirrel. She never cared what she looked like or if anyone thought she was pretty or not.

Then all of a sudden, in fifth grade, something changed.

For some reason, she stopped wearing blue jeans and boots and started wearing frilly little dresses.

If I close my eyes, I can still see that girl sitting in the cafeteria (which was outdoors, as many cafeterias in California's schools are). She used to watch boys take turns climbing a tree— which they had been warned repeatedly not to do. In fact, that girl even told the boys herself they were not supposed to climb the tree.

It wasn't that she minded what they were

70

doing. But she didn't like it that they could climb the tree and she couldn't.

She loved climbing trees. But she wore dresses now. "My tree climbing days are probably over," she thought. "I'm a girl, and girls aren't supposed to climb trees."

If you think it's weird that I know what this girl was thinking, you should know that I, Camy Baker, was that girl.

It frightened me to think about all this. It frightened me to realize I stopped singing songs in third grade because I cared too much about what other people thought. And in the fifth grade, I stopped climbing trees because I thought girls shouldn't climb trees.

What's next? What am I going to stop doing because I'm worried what other people might think? What am I going to stop doing because I think it's something a girl shouldn't do?

Writing?! But I love writing! As much as I used to love singing and climbing trees!

I stood up and started pacing my room, really upset. "I don't want to quit writing," I said to myself. "It's so important to me."

I started to panic. What if one day I just stopped writing—and I didn't know why!

I DIDN'T WANT TO LOSE ANYTHING ELSE IMPORTANT TO ME!!!!!

I started crying. Like *major* sob time.

Before I knew it, I bolted through Sara's bedroom door. "Sara!" I said. "I'm disappearing!"

Looking back, I realize I was being a drama princess, probably thanks to my hormones. Sara put down the book she was reading and took me in her arms. I sobbed for, like, five minutes.

My dad came to the door and asked what had happened. Sara said, "She's fine, Dad. I can handle this."

When I finally stopped crying, I sat up, suddenly feeling embarrassed about being so melodramatic. Sara didn't look at me like I was weird, though. In fact, she seemed to understand what I was feeling.

"Why do you feel like disappearing?" she asked me.

I told her everything. How every year it seemed like I'd lost more and more of the things I loved about myself. And I was frightened I would lose more things. I loved the things I loved, and I couldn't understand why I'd let them disappear.

Then the tears started again.

Sara sat there for a long time before she said anything. I could tell she was looking for just the right words. "Camy, you're becoming aware of yourself. You're becoming a woman. A lot of people are going to tell you what a woman should be. You might not know these people are influencing you, but they are. Now more than ever you have to pay attention to those influences."

"I don't get it," I said, sniffling.

"Who influences you most?"

" You and Mom, I guess."

"After us?" Sara asked.

"My friends?"

"Next?"

"My teachers?" I answered, and wondered if this was a test.

"And then . . . ?" she asked, like she was trying to lead me to something.

"But that's all!" I snapped, a little annoyed.

"Are you kidding?" she asked, and then laughed. "Who influences me? Mom? Your friends? Your teachers? Where do we get our ideas of what a woman should be?" She held out her hand and waved it around the room.

"Your room?" I asked, very annoyed. It seemed like she was making fun of me.

But then I looked around her room. Sara *was* leading me to something, and I finally understood.

I saw Sara's books. The covers of her CD's. Her movie posters. The television sitting in the corner. Her magazines. Her full-length mirror.

"The images," I said softly.

"Exactly," she said quietly, and slightly bowed her head, reminding me of Yoda from *Star Wars*.

I looked at the clock and saw it was almost ten-thirty. My brain was tired. My body was tired. I felt drained and wiped out. I desperately needed to get to sleep.

"Camy, now more than ever you have to pay attention to what's going on around you. And I'm not just saying with me, Mom, your friends, and your teachers. You've got to start paying attention to the images, too."

As I walked to her bedroom door, Sara said something I would never forget:

"Remember to stay true to yourself."

16

don't be a tv clone

ever since Sara and I had our talk, I have to admit that it became harder and harder for me to gain much pleasure from watching TV.

Don't get me wrong, I still enjoy TV. I mean, sometimes there's nothing better after a hard day at school than plopping down in front of the set and vegging out.

And my parents are pretty cool about TV and don't limit the time I watch it. I've figured out, though, they have tricks to keep me busy so I don't watch too much.

"Camy, it's time for homework."

"Camy, it's time to eat!"

"Camy, it's time to do the dishes!"

Camy this, Camy that! Gosh, can't a girl watch her favorite show in peace, for crying out loud?

Anyway, one day I was watching my favorite show. And I was paying a lot more attention than I normally do. In fact, I noticed something really peculiar. The lead actress seemed very familiar to me, like I knew her. In fact, she reminded me of a lot of girls who go to my school. It's weird, but I'd never really noticed that before.

I found myself thinking, "That's so cool. This actress is hip to what every girl at my school is wearing." Because her clothes were very similar to the ones they wear.

Then I found myself thinking, "That's so cool. This actress has the same haircut a lot of the girls at my school have. It's like she studied my school to gain more insight into the part!"

Then I found myself thinking, "It's really weird. This actress even acts like the girls at my school. What, does she have a miniature camera hidden somewhere at our school and, like, tapes us or something? I mean, she laughs just like the girls at my school laugh. She stands and walks and runs and dances like they do too."

That's when it hit me.

This actress wasn't copying the girls at my school.

The girls at my school were copying *her*.

To tell you the truth, it gave me the heebie-jeebies.

For a minute I felt like I had just uncovered a conspiracy. You know the feeling—everyone knows something that you don't.

So why didn't it ever occur to *me* to copy this actress?

Or was I copying her and not even realizing it?

After doing a mental check of my wardrobe, my hair, and my laugh, I realized I wasn't a clone yet.

But what about my friends?

Nope, Jackie's not like the actress. She's getting round and curvy like the actress, but her hair is totally different. And Jackie still loves overalls. This actress prefers really tight sweaters.

My friend Tammy is the *furthest* thing from this actress! In fact, Tammy might beat this actress up if she could because she can't stand china dolls, as Tammy calls them. (Tammy, needless to say, gets into a lot of trouble at school.)

My friend Rachel from Beverly Hills doesn't even watch TV. And if she did, I don't think she'd be impressed with this actress, considering her mom is a superstar and all.

But then something else hit me.

Most of the girls at school who reminded me of the actress were, like, a grade older than me or more.

"So is this what happens in seventh?" I wondered.

Not that all the girls in seventh grade and above are TV clones. But a lot of them are. And usually the cloning starts with one group of girls—the girls who think they're really popular.

It's like they turn on TV, find an actress the think is pretty (or who their boyfriends think is pretty), and copy her look exactly. And her mannerisms—you know, the way she acts.

After one group of girls completes the cloning, another group of girls becomes clones.

Then another group. 'Cause let's face it. Girls who hang out together like to look like each other. It makes them feel better or something.

Pretty soon everyone looks the same, and you have a hard time telling all the girls apart. Each girl looks like a clone of an actress on a TV show!

"Sick!" I thought.

If becoming a seventh-grader meant I had to become a clone, I decided I was going to go the other way. I'd shave my head and get a magnetic nose ring (you know, the kind where piercing isn't involved).

Not that I would actually do something as radical as that!

But now I know why some kids in my school dress so crazy.

They'd probably gotten the heebie-jeebies themselves, seeing all those girls turning into clones. They went anticlone to protect their identities!!!

And that's really what this rule is really all about.

As we move deeper into puberty, there's going to be more and more pressure on us to change our identities so we'll fit in with what other girls are doing.

But it's kind of depressing to realize clones

aren't doing anything original. They're just copying what they see on TV. How creative is that? Not very.

Since I'm an independent kind of girl, I've decided I might look to TV to get ideas on how to dress or act. But I am not going to copy anyone.

See, there's only one Camy Baker. But if this Camy Baker suddenly becomes like other girls, she might lose some of the things that are unique about her.

I, Camy Baker, have decided I'm going to shine in a crowd by being myself. And I hope you'll join me in being individual, special, and unique.

Anyway, I must have been on a roll that night. After watching my favorite show, I suddenly found myself staring at a bunch of lame commercials!

That's when I came up with the next rule!

become *super*aware of commercials

to tell you the truth, I never really paid much attention to commercials before.

Except for Gap ads, commercials are usually boring. Whenever my favorite TV show would break for a commercial, I'd just sit there with my eyes glazed over and wait until I heard the theme song of my show before I'd start to pay attention again.

It had never really dawned on me what kinds of messages those commercials were feeding me!

Let me give you some examples. Recently I saw three truly awful commercials in a row.

COMMERCIAL #1

A woman is sitting on a couch. The woman says guys are lucky because they can eat anything they want.

Next the woman introduces the product she's trying to sell—low-fat crackers. And she starts devouring them. It's like she's never eaten before in her life. But now that these low-fat crackers are here—and they *are* low in fat—she can eat like there's no tomorrow!

At the end of the commercial, after the woman has eaten every single crumb in the box, she says something like, "I wish I were a guy." Then she holds up the box of crackers and says, "No, I don't."

COMMERCIAL #2

A guy is making calls to a bunch of different girls. He's asking them all out on dates. These gorgeous women are in the shower, washing their hair with this new, wonderful shampoo.

The women are moaning like they're very, very excited. And the women keep saying they're too busy to go out.

Obviously, they're too busy to go out because washing their hair is such a great, sexy experience!

COMMERCIAL #3

The commercial starts with a song. The lyrics go something like, "Some guys have all the luck. . . ." Only the song is sung by a girl.

Then you see this really made-up woman, walking toward the camera like she's a cat.

She's eyeing something. And it's a guy.

Then you see the guy. He notices this really incredible girl coming toward him. And he's, like, stoked!

The guy wins some sort of prize offered by the soda company. And then the guy walks off really happy because he won. What was his prize? The girl!

Some seriously sick messages here! These commercials tap into our biggest fear—that if we're not beautiful, no one will want us.

A lot of the commercials we see have the some message. You have to be beautiful; you have to be thin; you have to be tan; you have to dress well; you have to make yourself even more beautiful than the other girls.

And commercials go by so quickly, we don't always pay close attention to what they're saying. This means they're affecting us without our realizing it!

That's called *brainwashing*!

When you see the same message over and over, you may start to believe it. You may feel that you're not beautiful enough, thin enough, tan enough, well dressed enough, or prettier than the other girls. In short, you may get the message: You're not good enough exactly the way you are.

If you start to believe this sick message, the brainwashing is complete.

Confidence is one of the most important things you can have while going through puberty. Confidence is the little voice inside your head that says, "You are wonderful exactly the way you are. You don't need to change. If others don't like you, it's their loss!"

Confidence encourages you to feel good about yourself.

But these sick commercials zap your confidence. They brainwash you into believing you can only feel good about yourself if you buy certain products. Sick commercials put pressure on you to pay more attention to the way you look. But I've already explained what happens when you do this. You become super-critical of yourself.

Well, no more, girls. I say, *Snap!* It's time we become supercritical of the people that are trying to brainwash us!

The best way to deal with a commercial is *not* to just sit there all glazed over and wait for it to pass. That's when the brainwashing begins.

You have to start becoming *really* aware of commercials. Every time you see a commercial, you have to ask: What technique are they using to get me to buy their product? Are they flattering me? Are they trying to scare me? Are they trying to make me think I'm not cool? Are they trying to make me think more boys will like me if I buy this product?

If the commercials you see aren't sending the message that you're a smart, wonderful, and amazing person, you need to do one simple thing.

You need to change the channel till *that* commercial is over.

Next rule!

try not to take fashion mags too seriously

next to television shows and commercials, fashion magazines are one of the most important influences on a girl when she's deciding how she should look.

Fashion magazines can be very helpful. They have great advice columns that give you a lot of information on things ranging from puberty to fashion to boys.

But these mags are also kind of bad for us if we take them too seriously. The reason?

Well, to start, we can look at those "in" and "out" lists most magazines include in each issue.

Let's use an example. Say you buy a pair of platform shoes you just love. But a fashion magazine suddenly puts platform shoes on the "out" list.

"Uh-oh," you think, "my most favorite platform shoes are out of style. I guess I can't wear them anymore."

Now you feel like you have to go out and buy a new pair of shoes—the kind that are suddenly "in," according to the magazine.

You see what just happened? The fashion magazine sold you a *new* pair of shoes by making you feel like your shoes were out of style.

It's a trick they use to keep you buying new stuff.

Some girls come from families with a lot of money. They can buy "in" stuff whenever the fashion magazines tell them to.

But girls like me, who have to pay for most of their shoes with a very small allowance, can't keep running out to buy trendy new stuff!

Why are fashion magazines so concerned about selling stuff? Well, the people who make the stuff pay a lot of money to run ads in the magazines.

The magazines need to keep those people happy so they'll buy more ads.

Have you ever heard the saying "you

scratch my back, and I'll scratch yours"? It means that if you do something for me, I'll do something for you. So people who make products like clothes and shoes take out ads in the magazines, and the magazines try to sell those products.

How does this rule relate to puberty?

Simple, really. As Sara said before, a lot of people are going to try to tell us what it means to be a woman.

But a lot of those people trying to influence us aren't being responsible enough to think about our feelings. I mean, if they cared about our feelings, they wouldn't try to make us feel bad for not buying "in" stuff.

Trust me. I know what it's like not to be able to afford the kinds of clothes other girls are wearing. Why do you think I got creative and started thrift shopping? The truth: I couldn't afford designer labels! And in Beverly Hills, you can't wear a shirt that looks *similar* to a designer shirt. You have to wear *the* designer shirt, or you're not cool.

Well, I turned that silly concept all around. I proved coolness with my creativity. I got away from the herd by being smart. And you can too.

There's no reason you should feel bad about yourself just the way you are. If you read a fashion magazine and start feeling bad because all the girls seem to know what's "in" except you, you're not alone. Most girls reading the magazine don't really know what's going on either! They can only copy what they see, which isn't very original.

Now, I'm not saying you should cancel your subscriptions to all your favorite magazines, or stop reading fashion magazines.

All I'm saying is that if you get the feeling they're pressuring you to be something you're not, just ignore the fashion trends they show.

Always remember that it's not important to worry about being what everyone thinks is cool. It's more important to remember to be *you*.

And trust me—being you is a whole lot cooler than copying your look from a magazine! ☺

it's okay if you don't look like a model

In the previous rule, I talked a little bit about fashion magazines. Now it's time to talk about another thing that has a lot of influence on us: models.

A lot of girls I know want to look like models. In fact, a lot of girls I know want to *be* models. Hey, even *I* wouldn't mind being a model.

In fact, I have to admit something kind of embarrassing. Recently I read in a fashion magazine that one of the world's largest modeling agencies was looking for new models. They were looking for girls between the ages of thirteen and seventeen who were at least five feet, nine inches tall.

I didn't exactly fit what they were looking for, but I sent my picture in anyway.

Don't laugh! I love being a writer. But I wouldn't mind being a supermodel. *Hello!* How cool would *that* be? Or that's the way I used to think.

Anyway, a few months passed and I never heard back from the agency. "How rude," I thought. I went to all the trouble of sending them my photo. The least they could do is call me back to thank me for it!

All of a sudden I got panicked. *Am* I ugly?

I started looking at the pictures in the fashion magazines and realized I didn't look *anything* like those models.

In horror, I realized the awful truth.

I *am* ugly!

The moment I realized this, I started crying. (Looking back, I attribute it to hormones.) But at the time I felt really freaked out, and even a little angry.

So I pulled out my cordless phone and called information to get the number of that modeling agency. Then I called them.

I explained to the receptionist that I was a twelve-year-old girl from Peoria who wrote books and that they were mean, and that I was going to write something really bad about them if they didn't put someone on the phone to tell me why they thought I was ugly.

And I was crying the whole time.

Well, the lady put me on hold. Then this other lady picked up and calmed me down. She was really nice. I explained to her that I was just feeling vulnerable and emotional. She said she understood.

To make a long story short, the woman agreed to let me interview her for this book. So, in a way, I was going to kill two birds with one stone (not that I advocate killing of any sort!) by getting an interview and also learning why the agency never called me back.

It took me about a week to get my interview questions together.

Then I called the woman at the agency, Mary Ellen Baker (no relation!), for the interview. (I also re-sent my picture to Mary Ellen, just in case she couldn't find the first one!)

INTERVIEW WITH MARY ELLEN BAKER

CAMY: Thank you so much for taking the time to speak with me. I hear

	the phones ringing off the hook in the background, so you must be busy!
MARY ELLEN:	Very. But this is an important issue to discuss, so it's my pleasure.
CAMY:	The first time we spoke, I mentioned that I sent my picture to your agency and never got a call back. Is that pretty standard?
MARY ELLEN:	Absolutely. First of all, let me start by saying that we get over a thousand picture submissions every week.
CAMY:	A thousand a week! Yikes!
MARY ELLEN:	So you understand there is no way for us to respond personally to every submission.
CAMY:	That's a lot of photos.
MARY ELLEN:	Right. There's only one person in the mailroom who handles all that mail. Thank you for re-sending your picture, by the way. You look adorable. I love that outfit!
CAMY:	Thanks! Okay, so be honest. What are my chances of becoming a model?

MARY ELLEN:	*(laughs)* Unfortunately, Camy, you just aren't tall enough. You are a beautiful girl, but unless you grow to be five feet nine, it's unlikely you can be a model.
CAMY:	Ouch.
MARY ELLEN:	Let me explain a little how the process works. At our agency, as with most agencies, we look for very specific things. For us to consider signing a girl up, she has to be at least five feet, nine inches tall.
CAMY:	Can't you consider someone who's five feet four?
MARY ELLEN:	Fashion designers work with a set standard when they create the clothes for the photo shoots and fashion shows. It doesn't mean the clothes won't be made into different sizes later. But at the beginning, it's easier for the designers to work with one set standard, which is what we have today. This doesn't mean girls

should feel bad about themselves if they are not five feet nine. Most girls are *not* this height. Models aren't better because they're tall. They simply fit the clothes!

CAMY: So why five nine? That seems pretty random!

MARY ELLEN: In fact, the average height of models used to be much less. But that was back in the days when models only showed clothes for a very small, intimate audience— maybe fifteen or twenty people. Height wasn't as important then. Today models show clothes for huge audiences. If you've ever watched the E! or VH-1 fashion shows, you can see that the audience is filled with hundreds and hundreds of people. The taller a girl is, the more she'll stand out on the runway.

CAMY: Or on the basketball team or volleyball team.

MARY ELLEN: Exactly. Height is as important for modeling as it is for certain sports.

CAMY: So how important are looks? Don't you have to be, like, incredibly gorgeous to be a model?

MARY ELLEN: Not necessarily. One thing many girls don't understand is that a lot of work goes into making a model look the way she does. Remember this: Models have makeup artists who do their makeup. Models have hairstylists who do their hair. Models have people who create special lighting when their picture is taken. You and I don't have those things. If we did, we would look like models too!

CAMY: Why do you think a lot of girls are so interested in becoming models?

MARY ELLEN: I think a lot of girls are infatuated with modeling because today's models are celebrities. We all have that tiny part of us that thinks being famous would be really fun. But if one wants to become famous, one can be an actress, a singer, an athlete, a fashion designer—or a writer like you, Camy.

CAMY: All they have to is work at it!

MARY ELLEN: Exactly. Girls see modeling as something easy and glamorous, but you cannot imagine the work that goes into it. And traveling might sound fun, but the fun wears off very quickly. Most models spend much time away from the people they love. And many, many models have dreams of doing other things, like acting or singing or writing. For them, modeling is just a way to get into other things.

CAMY: Okay, one more question: Why are models all so skinny? I'm skinny myself, but I know a lot of girls who aren't. And they think they should be skinny 'cause their favorite model is.

MARY ELLEN: That's a great question. The modeling world gets a lot of criticism for showing mostly very thin girls. There is a movement now to include a broader range of body sizes, but it's going to take a while.

CAMY: Pretend for a moment I *am* five nine. How thin would I have to be to become a model?

MARY ELLEN: I am not going to lie to you and say that a model's weight doesn't matter. It is important, but there's absolutely no exact right or wrong weight. It all depends on the shape of a girl's body. In the modeling world, we look for girls who are a specific height. *That* is the most important quality.

I never encourage my models to diet to lose weight. I try to get them focused on being healthy, eating natural foods, and exercising moderately. When girls cut back on food to lose weight, they don't look healthy. They develop bags under their eyes, and their hair becomes brittle. Makeup can *hide* these problems, but it doesn't *solve* them. And I don't feel right encouraging a girl to become something she isn't.

In life, there are all types of bodies. Tall and thin, short and round. Tall and round, short and thin, et cetera. Your body knows how it wants to be. When you try to make it something it isn't, through diet or cosmetic surgery or whatever, it doesn't look natural. A natural, healthy body is the most beautiful body, whatever its shape. It's really a gift.

CAMY: Well, you've answered all my questions. I won't lie and say I'm not disappointed 'cause I'm not going to be a model, but at least I understand now. I do have one final question.

Obviously, height is the most important thing in becoming a model. But I've often read about girls who model. They say that in school they were teased and ridiculed because they were so tall. Can you tell my readers how important it is *not* to be mean to a girl because she's tall?

MARY ELLEN: I think you said it perfectly yourself.

CAMY'S NOTE:

So there you have it. My modeling career is officially over before it began! Am I bummed? Yeah. Oh well, *c'est la vie!* (That's French for "That's life.")

Anyway, try not to feel bad if you're never going to be a model. You're in really, *really* good company! ☺

20
choose to be beautiful

even though I'll never be a model, that doesn't mean I still don't want to be beautiful!

Let's face it. Most of us, for whatever reason, would like to be beautiful.

The only problem is, no one tells us what being beautiful really means. Sure, television and magazines try to tell us what a beautiful person *should* look like. Just because they show us a person *they* think is beautiful, that doesn't really explain what beauty is.

To get to the root of this beauty problem, I decided to define beauty for myself. First I had to find the prettiest girl I knew. Then I had to figure out what made her beautiful.

My friend Regan from Beverly Hills is the prettiest girl I know. To give you a little history about our relationship, you should know that Regan and I used to be enemies. I always thought she was very controlling toward her friends and mean to everyone else.

She had her problems with me, too. She thought I was too peppy and that I was stuck-up.

I guess you'd say we just could *not* get along. (We've made up, though, and now we're becoming closer and closer friends!)

Anyway, I've always thought Regan was *very* pretty. And not only is she pretty, but she wears the most expensive clothes you could ever want. She has her hair done twice a month at a fancy salon on Rodeo Drive. Once a week she has her nails done. She even gets a facial every once in a while!

In terms of looks, you'll probably never find a girl who's prettier than Regan.

The funny thing is, I really couldn't bring myself to say that Regan was beautiful.

In fact, I started thinking of other people in my life who I thought were more beautiful. Like my best friend, Jackie. Or my older sister,

Sara. My mom is definitely one of the most beautiful people in the world to me.

This really tripped me out. I asked my mom why I was having this dilemma.

"You remember that saying 'Beauty is in the eye of the beholder'?" my mom asked.

"Yeah."

"Well, what does it mean to you?"

"It means that beauty is different for each person. What one person thinks is beautiful, another person might not."

"Exactly. So what is beautiful to you?"

I had to think about it, but not long. The answer was on the tip of my tongue. "Things that make me happy are very beautiful."

"Does Regan make you happy?"

"Sometimes. I like the new Regan—she makes me happy. But there's still some of the old Regan there, and that doesn't make me happy."

"So she's on her way to becoming beautiful, but she isn't there yet in your opinion?"

"Exactly!"

And that's when it hit me.

Beauty isn't what you *see*. Beauty is what you *feel*. We can all be beautiful. We *are* all beautiful. But we have to choose to see that beauty.

It's hard to choose to be beautiful when you think beauty can be bought off the rack, or found in a bottle of makeup or at a plastic surgeon's office.

The thinking goes, "I have to buy the best clothes to be beautiful." Or "I have to have the best hair, skin, and makeup to be beautiful." Or "I have to have my nose fixed to be beautiful." If you're looking for beauty as something you can buy, you're looking in the wrong place. All you have to do is look inside.

Beauty can't be packaged, bought, or sold. Beauty starts from the inside—when you have a positive attitude about yourself and the world around you.

I'm not saying you have to use *my* definition of beauty. In fact, no one can tell you how to define beauty. Only you can define beauty. 'Cause beauty *is* in the eye of the beholder. And you're the beholder! That means *you* decide what you think is beautiful, no one else.

But I must warn you. If you think beauty is something that can be packaged, bought, or sold, you might have trouble following the next rule:

stay out of the beauty war

the beauty war is the competition a girl feels to be the prettiest girl in school.

Now, I like competitions. (I recently won a spelling bee and loved every second of it!) But the beauty war is something that can *never* be won.

The other bad thing about the beauty war is that you're giving some of your power away by (1) being jealous of another girl; (2) comparing yourself to another girl; and (3) disliking another girl because you're afraid she might be prettier than you. Not to mention that competing to be the prettiest girl in school can take up a whole lot of your time!

Let me give you an example. There's a girl at Peoria Middle School named Christi, an eighth-grader who was recently voted Best-Looking Girl for our yearbook.

It might sound like she won the beauty war, right? Wrong! Read on!

Christi is a very pretty girl, though I personally believe she would be a lot prettier if she didn't wear so much makeup. But she's so preoccupied with her looks that I can't imagine her having time to do anything else but put on makeup!

I'm not kidding. Every morning when I see Christi, she is so "done up"—her hair is perfect, her makeup is perfect, her clothes are perfect—that I have the sneaking suspicion she started getting ready for school the night before!

I often run into Christi in the girls' bathroom. She's either putting on more mascara or spraying her hair to hold it in place. And she sure needs that hairspray! 'Cause the way that girl styles her hair totally defies gravity!

My best friend, Jackie, and I usually sit at a table close to Christi and her friends at lunch. Because Jackie and I are lowly sixth-graders, Christi and her friends don't pay much attention to us. And that's a *good* thing, because

Christi and her friends don't seem to like any girls outside their group. There's one girl in particular, Michelle, who Christi and her friends *really* seem to hate. From what other kids have told me, Christi and her friends don't even *know* Michelle.

So why do they hate her? Well, according to my sources, Michelle came very close to winning the Best-Looking Girl contest. It sounds like Christi and her friends hate Michelle because she's pretty too.

Since Christi is competing in the beauty war, she hates other pretty girls who might threaten her. The funny thing is, Michelle doesn't even care about the war!

I actually had a chance to meet Michelle at a school pep rally when I sat next to her in the bleachers. And she's a very nice girl. Unlike Christi, Michelle doesn't seem preoccupied with her looks. You can tell she feels confident about being pretty simply because she's secure about her looks. Christi, on the other hand, is very insecure about her looks. Why else does she spend so much time getting ready every day?!

If you're the kind of girl who thinks you can only look good if you spend a lot of money on makeup, the best clothes, or expensive dye jobs at a ritzy salon, you really need to pay attention to this rule. Because according to my research, girls who put too much emphasis on their looks and clothes are not as happy as girls who accept themselves as they are.

Besides, it takes a lot of time and energy to make yourself look really made up. And when you spend that much time trying to improve your looks, you become so preoccupied that you think less and less about other people. I don't care who you ask. I doubt you'll find anyone who thinks selfishness is beautiful.

I really, truly believe you should stay out of the beauty war. It's what my dad calls a losing battle—a fight you cannot win.

But if you try to fight the beauty war, you might lose a lot: your time, your money, and your *very* valuable energy.

22

look good for you, not boys

television shows, commercials, magazines, and other girls aren't the only ones who are going to have an influence on how you think you should look.

Boys are going to have a lot of influence on you too. Have you ever noticed that the older we get, the more important boys' opinions of us seem to become?

Don't get me wrong. I know it's nice to be admired. Even though one boy called me a spider, boys have shown that they're interested in me. It feels good when boys pay attention to me.

But I don't purposely dress myself up to attract boys, that's for sure! The reason? I've seen what happens when girls in my school spend so much time worrying about how they look just to get the attention of guys.

The sad thing about that type of girl is that she always needs a boy to pay attention to her to believe she looks good.

And then what happens when the guy she likes doesn't pay attention to her? I'll tell you what happens.

She gets depressed. She thinks she must not be very pretty. She might even totally convince herself that she's ugly! Just because *one* boy didn't pay attention to her!

It makes me very sad when I see a girl who thinks the only thing she has to offer a potential boyfriend is her looks.

I understand why some girls feel this way. It goes back to the brainwashing we receive from commercials. It's like we're programmed to think: You must be gorgeous or no boy will want you.

But think about this: Say you get a boyfriend because he thinks you're hot. What then?

If he only likes you because you're cute, where is the relationship going to go? I'll tell you: nowhere fast!

I'm not saying you shouldn't try to look good. There's nothing wrong with looking good! I *am* saying you shouldn't depend on a boy's approval to *believe* you look good. Choose to look good for *you*. Chances are, boys are going to find your self-confidence a heck of a lot more attractive than just the way you look.

Trust me. The kind of boy worth attracting is a boy who likes the *whole* you. Not only your looks, but your intelligence, feelings, and personality too.

The great thing is, all you have to do to attract that kind of boy is be yourself! ☺

23

protect your power

you might not climb trees anymore.
And you might not sing cute little songs.

Maybe you wear dresses and makeup and like pretty clothes.

Maybe boys are very important to you.

Maybe you like what you see on TV.

And maybe you want to be a model like the ones you see in magazines.

But this I know, and I hope you learn it too: There's something very special about you.

I *really* hope you live in a nice world where everyone around you supports your power. That means everyone accepts you for who you are.

They don't ask you to change into something you don't want to be.

You'll know when you are in your power because you'll feel good about yourself. Your light is on and it's shining brightly.

But if you ever find yourself feeling down, and following all these rules doesn't help— don't despair.

The reason for it just might be that you're having a hard time protecting your power.

What that means is, someone or something is encouraging you to feel bad about yourself. And you don't know how to stop them from influencing you.

But protecting your power is actually very, very easy.

Let's say you're watching TV. And a show comes on that you don't like. It's either boring, scary, or stupid.

So you pick up the remote and change the channel.

Basically, you took your attention away from something you didn't like and searched for something a little better.

You just *ZAPPED* it right out of your mind.

Well, this is what you do with anything that messes with your power.

Before you can protect your power, though, you have to realize who or what is messing with it.

Let me use an example.

Remember that kid I mentioned who called me a spider? Well, the guy uses "Spider" as my nickname now. Fortunately, after the talk I had with my mom, I realized I'd let that boy's comment take my power away. Well, no more!

When that boy calls me Spider, here's what I do: I turn my back and forget all about him.

I have just taken away his power over me.

TV shows, commercials, girls who are mean, boys who try to make you feel unattractive— *all* these influences might try to make you think something negative about yourself.

But you've got the power, girl! *You* can decide how you feel.

The best way to protect your power is to focus on the things that make you happy, and to turn your attention away from the things that don't make you happy.

But you have to pay close attention. You have to find out what makes you happy and what doesn't.

A lot of times you'll discover this: The things that make you happy are the things that encourage you to be *you*.

The things that make you unhappy are the things that don't accept you for who you are. Or the things that influence you to be something you don't feel comfortable being.

You'll know the difference between the two. All you have to do is keep your eyes open and struggle to remain true to yourself.

As for the boy who calls me Spider, I *could* get really mad. I could say, "You better leave me alone or I'm going to tell!"

But I don't want to stoop to his level. Sure, it stings at first when I hear him say, "Hey, Spider. Kill any flies today?"

But as soon as I walk away, I forget all about him.

Always remember: Your own personal power is the good feelings you have about yourself.

These positive feelings of power are like a little treasure.

And like any treasure, it needs to be protected. It's up to you to protect your power.

24

communicate with your parents

just for the record, my mom didn't force me to write this rule! I came up with it on my own!

This rule is really important. Because as we are changing, our relationships with our parents are changing too.

See, as we're slowly changing into adults, we're also beginning the process of developing our own identities. Part of developing our own identities means distancing ourselves from our parents. That's a key part of growing up! It doesn't mean we don't love our parents. All it means is that we're trying to figure out who *we* are!

You might find yourself pulling away from

your parents—you know, spending more time alone in your room or with your friends. Or maybe you don't like asking for your parents' opinion on things as much as you used to. And certainly it might irritate you if your parents always tell you what to do, like you're still a little kid.

Always remember, though, your parents can be the best and most valuable source of information you'll ever have.

I know it can be hard talking to your parents when you're going through puberty. And from what Sara tells me, it gets harder the older you get. You don't want their advice anymore because you want to make your own decisions.

But remember, that your parents have a lot more experience than you. They have wisdom we don't yet have. Instead of ignoring their wisdom or not asking for it, we can save ourselves a lot of time by getting the answers we need from someone who's been through a lot of what we're just starting to go through.

I think a lot of kids are afraid to talk to their parents about puberty for one simple reason: They don't want to talk to their parents about sex. I mean, how embarrassing can it be to have to sit there and listen to your mom (or maybe your dad) talk about sex?

I was browsing through a Web site and came across a message board filled with postings girls had put up about puberty.

One girl asked, "What's the best way to talk to 'rents about stuff? Not sex, though, but shaving, etc."

The way she asked the question confirmed my suspicion: "This girl has some important questions, but she doesn't want to ask them because she's afraid of the big sex lecture."

I consulted my mom about this one. "If I asked you about shaving my legs, would you try to tell me about sex?"

My mom sat silent for a moment, then said, "Well, shaving is a sign that you're getting closer to your period. And when you get your period, it's closer to the time to talk about sex so you are educated about the choices. So, yes, I might bring it up."

"But don't you think we should talk about it when I'm ready? Not when you think it's time?"

"That's a good question. I never really thought about that."

"Happy to be of help," I said.

One thing I've learned about my mom is that she really wants to make sure I'm as well informed about the world as possible. I appreciate that, I really do.

But, well, sometimes she can drop a whole lot of information on me at one time. I mean, who wants a lecture? We get enough lectures at school. Am I right?

So here's what I've decided for myself, and maybe you can try this too.

If you have a puberty question you'd like to ask your mom or dad, ask the question.

But be *really* specific. Don't ask more than one question. Take it one step at a time. For instance, if you want to know about shaving, go to your mom (or I guess your dad, too, if you want) and say, "I think it's time for me to start shaving. How do I do it?"

Hopefully, your mom or dad will tell you all you need to know about shaving and leave it at that.

But if they say, "I guess now is the time for *the* talk" (you know which talk they mean—the *sex* talk), here's what I suggest you do.

Tell them the following line (and try to

memorize it if you can): "I am not ready for any more information right now. After all, shaving is a big step. It's better to handle one big step at a time!"

Trust me, your parents will appreciate the fact that you're not ready to talk about sex yet. (They might even be relieved! My mom swears it's not easy for parents to give that lecture. They feel as uncomfortable as we do!)

And I bet if you let your parents know that you value their advice but you need to take it at your own pace, they'll be very pleased you're being so mature.

What's more important, though, is that you're going to gain confidence in your ability to ask intelligent questions. Not only that, you're going to stay in control by setting some very specific limits and boundaries. You're saying, "I know what questions I have, and I know when the time is right for me to ask them."

If you practice asking questions this way, I can almost guarantee that it will become easier and easier to talk to your parents about other things. Maybe after some practice, you might even find you can talk to your parents about sex without getting grossed out and embarrassed.

But when you do feel comfortable enough to talk to your parents about sex, don't tackle the whole subject all at once.

Remember: Ask one question at a time. That way, you'll be able to get the answers you're comfortable with and ready for.

help your sister

if your school is anything like mine, it has tons of cliques—groups of girls who hang out together.

I personally am not in a clique. I hang out mostly with my best friend, Jackie. Of course we have tons of other friends, but we try to stay away from cliques.

The reason? To be honest, cliques bother me. It's like girls in a clique don't think it's possible to walk from one class to another class unless they're surrounded by a thousand other girls.

And remember what I said earlier about how girls in a clique start to dress, act, and sound the same?

Now, I'm not saying that if you're in a clique, you're doing something wrong. If you like being in a clique, then I say more power to you, girl.

But just because you're in a clique doesn't mean you should treat girls outside the clique badly.

Trust me. I know what it feels like to be treated badly by a clique.

There was a clique at Beverly Hills Elementary run by my former enemy, Regan. The girls in this clique could be really mean to girls outside the group. Why? I really don't know. But it seems like some girls think just because they're in a clique, they're better than other people.

Anyway, one time I got a taste of how mean girls in a clique can really be. I can't remember how it all started, but Regan decided that she and the other girls in her group weren't speaking to me. Every girl in the clique ignored me, and this abuse lasted for about a week. At first my feelings were really hurt. I had no idea what I had done to deserve that kind of treatment. But after a few days it really didn't matter. I never hung out with any of those girls to begin with, and I still had my true friends.

Still! It was a very mean thing to do.

We need to remember that puberty isn't easy. While most girls make it through puberty with their butterfly wings intact, all this changing can be pretty rough on us.

And you can't tell me that even if you're in a clique, puberty isn't difficult for you.

So why can't we help each other through this difficult time? Why can't we treat each other like sisters? 'Cause as girls, we're *all* sisters.

If you are in a clique, don't be mean to the girls who aren't part of it. You'd only be doing it to fit in with those who enjoy hurting other people. There's nothing cool about that. I know you might feel pressured to go along with the crowd. But you are responsible for the way *you* treat other people. It's up to you to be nice to people, even if those in your clique are not.

I'm not saying you have to hang out with girls you don't want to hang out with. But I truly believe girls should be nice to *all* girls.

Just because we aren't all friends doesn't mean we can't all be friendly.

Who knows? Maybe one day when you need it, someone outside your clique will be friendly to *you*.

be creative

Some girls go through puberty without any problems at all. Their weight isn't a problem. Their skin never breaks out. Their breasts grow evenly and are neither too big nor too small.

They aren't so tall that they tower over all the kids—boys included. And they aren't so small that they get lost in the crowd.

These girls have parents who are understanding and protective, yet allow them room to grow. These girls are accepted in school. And they value themselves as beautiful, smart, and wonderful people.

If you're like the girls I've just described, I'm

very happy for you. I'm glad your transition through puberty has been an easy one.

But maybe your puberty isn't going so great.

Maybe your parents aren't treating you well and you feel misunderstood.

Maybe you don't even *have* parents.

Maybe other kids treat you badly.

Maybe you feel like no one in the world understands you.

Maybe you feel like other girls have everything and you have nothing because your family is poor.

No matter what you're going through, you have something within you that will make you feel better: your creativity.

Your creativity is the thing you use when you paint or draw or write or sing or make music. You use your creativity when you sculpt or knit or carve.

Your creativity is like a muscle. The more you use it, the stronger it becomes. But it's not the only thing that gets stronger. *You* become stronger too, when you discover a creative talent.

Of course you don't have to be going through a rough time before you start using your creativity. You should use your creativity whenever you can!

But if you *are* going through a hard time, developing your creativity can really help you feel better.

The truth is, some of the best works of art have been created by people who have had great struggles. These people developed their creativity as a way to take their mind off their worries. The best example I can share with you is *The Diary of Anne Frank*.

The Diary of Anne Frank is one of the best books I have ever read in my life. If you haven't read it yet, I strongly encourage you to read it as soon as possible.

Anne Frank was a girl who had to hide inside an office building in Holland during World War II. Anne Frank and her family were Jewish. They were hiding from the Nazis, who wanted to kill them.

When I say Anne Frank had to hide inside an office building, I don't mean she had a whole building. She had to stay in six tiny rooms that were hidden above the actual offices. And she shared this small space with seven other people. She and her family hid in these tiny rooms for two years, and they all had to be very quiet. If anyone found out they were there, they would all be taken away by the Nazis.

On top of all this, Anne Frank was going through puberty.

Despite how incredibly sad it was to learn what happened to Anne Frank, reading *The Diary of Anne Frank* was a very positive experience for me. To know a girl could create such a beautiful book under such horrendous circumstances was very humbling.

Anne Frank helped me realize that while puberty can be difficult, through creativity it can be turned into a beautiful, wonderful, and uplifting experience—no matter how bad the situation you find yourself in.

You and I will probably never have to suffer the pain that Anne Frank suffered. But through her struggles, we can learn that no matter how difficult our lives may be, we can use our creativity to make something beautiful out of any experience.

give every class your best effort

When writing a book about puberty, you have to do a *lot* of research. And you have to wade through a lot of information. One of the more interesting pieces of information was this:

I learned that some girls' grades drop when they start middle school or junior high.

Obviously, I was very curious.

I asked Sara if this had happened to her. She told me that while her grades didn't drop, certain subjects seemed to be a lot more challenging. "A lot of my friends started getting frustrated," she said, "and some of them stopped trying."

Hearing this, I started thinking about my

friends. Are there any girls I know who are getting frustrated with school?

Asking this question actually made me take a closer look at myself.

I don't like algebra. I don't like all those rules you have to remember. I know that sounds kind of weird coming from a girl who wrote a book filled with thirty rules!!!

But honestly, I am much more interested in English than algebra. I like English. English is easy for me. I'm going to (hopefully) make a lot more money later in life with my English skills than with my algebra skills.

Still, I give algebra the same effort I give English. Why?

Let's face it. There are certain things we like to study in school, and there are certain things we don't have a lot of interest in. But we can't choose *all* our classes. Some classes we just *have* to take.

But if we put our energy only into the classes we like, we might get a pretty messed-up report card: A, C, A, C. "How can I get an A in one class, but a C in the other?" you might ask yourself.

It's simple. You're trying harder in one class than in the other.

I know it's a challenge. But try to remain involved in every class you have, even the ones you don't like. Chances are, you don't like the class because it's not as easy for you as other classes. But that's why it's a challenge. Go for the challenge!

Even if you don't think you understand what's going on in class, you probably do. It might take a while for all the information you're learning to make sense, but that's okay. What doesn't make sense to you now will totally make sense to you soon, as long as you're still paying attention in class.

Another thing you should try to do is speak up in class. Ask questions. That'll help you stay involved. If you're having a hard time keeping up with the pace of the class, others probably are too.

Don't worry about aceing every single test. Just give the test your best effort. Your grades don't really show how smart you are. After all, you can be good at one subject and not so good at another. So don't despair if you don't always get an A.

But the classes you find more difficult are going to require a little more of your courage and your confidence.

So try to give each class your best effort before you give up. Okay?

look for positive role models

this rule was inspired by an assignment we had at school. The assignment was to pick a celebrity we admired and write a letter telling them how much they inspired us.

It took me a few days to narrow my list down. I had a really hard time choosing. Chelsea Clinton. Barbara Walters. Madonna. Rosie O'Donnell. Janet Reno. Maya Angelou. Dear Abby. Jewel. Judy Blume. Oh, the choices! So many different women and girls have inspired me in so many different ways!

Finally, though, I chose a woman I wanted to be like, some day. This woman is rich, classy, beautiful, intelligent, real, and honest. More importantly, she runs a successful media empire—which happens to be my very own goal!!!

My choice was Oprah Winfrey.

I wrote Oprah Winfrey a letter and told her how much I admired her for all these qualities. Although I haven't heard back from her yet, I expect a letter shortly!

The most important reason Oprah has inspired me is because of her amazing success. She gives me hope that I, too, can accomplish everything I want to accomplish.

Women like Oprah Winfrey stand as reminders that we can shoot for the stars—and reach them.

Anyone you admire and want to be like can be a role model; it doesn't have to be a celebrity or a woman. And you might find that your role models change. After all, you're changing, so the things you admire will change as well.

But I encourage you to find out as much as possible about your role model. If it's someone you know, ask them about their life. What lessons have they learned? What advice can they give you?

If your role model is someone like Oprah Winfrey—a person you don't know—I suggest you look for books and magazine stories about this person. Find out all about your role model. Let your role model's struggles teach you. And let your role model's successes inspire you.

Always remember: You can be anything you want to be. All you need to do is *believe* you can.

You *go,* girl!

discover new interests

I know a lot of girls who aren't really sure what they're interested in. Let's use my friend Sheila as an example. Here's a typical day in Sheila's life: She goes to school, comes home and does her homework, talks to friends on the phone, eats dinner, and watches TV before going to bed.

And Sheila tells me all the time, "I wish I had more things to do. I get so bored sometimes!"

So I asked her, "Well, what about hobbies? What interests you?"

And she's like, "I just don't know. I'm interested in boys, but that's about it!"

And I said, "Boys aren't hobbies. You gotta

135

figure out something else you like and start learning about it." And then I offered to go to the library with her to help figure out what her interests are. But she just wasn't interested in developing new interests.

Finally, one day after listening to Sheila sighing and griping because her life was so boring, I had finally had it. I told her, "Either come to the library with me this Saturday and we'll try to figure out what interests you, or quit complaining about your boring life, 'cause I'm sick of hearing about it!"

Not that I was trying to be mean or anything. I was just trying to prod her into going to the library with me. And it worked. The following Saturday we went down to Peoria Public Library. Sheila was dragging her feet, saying she was bored and she was going to miss all her Saturday-afternoon shows.

Well, about thirty minutes after we started exploring the library, Sheila found a big, glossy book on the Academy Awards that she seemed to really like. "You're gonna be okay?" I asked. "You're not going to die of boredom if I go look around?"

Sheila was so engrossed in the book she

didn't hear me, so I left her to do some exploring on my own. When I came back, she was halfway through the book, and she was totally excited. She loves watching the Academy Awards every year on television, and this book gave her a lot of new, cool information. She decided to check the book out of the library.

We did some more exploring, and Sheila found a book about sharks. She had always been fascinated by sharks—she watches Shark Week on the Discovery Channel every year. I was surprised how much she knew about sharks: how some are man-eaters and some are gentle giants like the whale shark, which is totally huge but eats only tiny plankton. Sheila checked the shark book out too, happy to realize that her fascination with sharks could be turned into a new interest.

It's been a few months since our excursion to the library, and Sheila's turning into quite an Academy Awards and shark trivia buff. Ask her any question about either subject and she'll probably have the right answer. Sheila, who never had a clue before what she wanted to do with herself later in life, now wants to be either a movie producer or a marine biologist. It's exciting to see her become more and more confident about herself as she learns more and more about the things that interest her. She's filling her mind with knowledge, but she's also having fun!

This rule relates to puberty for one important reason: Keeping busy with things that interest you is the best way to keep from stressing out because of all the changes you're going through. You know what I'm saying? The more interests you have in your life, the less time you're going to sit around worrying or being bored.

But more importantly, discovering new interests helps you feel more confident about yourself. When you have confidence, you have power.

'Nough said. ☺

30

the final rule

As we become young adults on our way to becoming women, we'll be faced with many people—friends, boyfriends, parents, teachers, actors, models, singers—who will influence and inspire us in many different ways. These people will influence what we wear, how we act, and even how we feel.

But part of becoming an adult means making choices for yourself. It means developing your own identity and becoming the adult you want to become.

I hope, I hope, I hope that as you become an adult, you always remain true to the girl you are now—the girl filled with power. Because we really *do* live in a world where it's possible to be anything you want to be and to accomplish anything you want to accomplish.

You're filled with electricity, girl. You really do have the power.

And my final rule is simply this:

Never let your power go.

2 **part** two

q: I get sick a lot and I'm not sure why. My mom tells me I'm imagining it. This makes me so mad! Sometimes I feel like I'm dying, and she'll totally blow it off and refuse to take me to the emergency room. Why is she so evil?!

a: This one I had to get some help with. First of all, the most important thing I want to say is that you have to trust your body. If you don't feel well, you don't feel well.

We all have times when we don't feel well. That's a natural part of puberty and life. But if you keep getting sick, you need attention.

If your mom doesn't give it to you, it doesn't mean she's evil. It just means she isn't recognizing the problem. Maybe because she doesn't see you vomiting, or bleeding, or losing or gaining weight (which are only a few possible symptoms of an illness), she doesn't believe you're sick.

Some people need proof that someone is ill before they'll believe it. Or maybe your mom thinks you're pretending to be sick to get attention.

But *you* are listening to your body. And it is telling you that you don't feel well. And you have to trust your body.

The first step you need to take is to write out your symptoms. Try to be as specific as possible.

Why don't you feel well? Do you hurt anywhere? Where do you hurt? Is it a general feeling of being sick? Or are there definitely things that you can see on your body that make you feel or think you're sick? Write everything out you possibly can about how you're feeling.

The next thing I want you to do is take this list to your school nurse. School nurses are not only there to fix cuts and bruises and give us tampons. They also help kids who aren't feeling well.

Hopefully, your school nurse will be able to help you sort out what's going on with your body.

q: Why do people say, "You need to get your beauty sleep"? And why do people say it to girls and not boys?

a: That's a great question. I think people tell girls they need to get their beauty sleep because there's a lot of pressure on us to be beautiful. Hopefully, this book addresses that whole beauty issue. I hope you know that beauty is something inside. You are already, if you choose to see it, very beautiful.

That said, sleep is *definitely* one of the most important things you can do to keep your body in tip-top shape.

Like water, food, and physical activity, sleep is something your body absolutely has to have.

When you sleep, your body rejuvenates itself. That's why people call it beauty sleep. When you get plenty of sleep, your body feels better. And as I've said time and time again, the best way to look good is to feel good.

You might find that you need more sleep when you're going through puberty. You might even find yourself napping when you come home from school. That's totally cool.

But if you find yourself feeling tired all the time, even if you're getting plenty of sleep and also napping quite a bit, I strongly suggest you talk to your school nurse or your family doctor.

The reason you're feeling tired could be that you could have an iron deficiency. That means you're not getting enough iron from the foods you eat. This is a somewhat common thing girls experience during puberty. Or maybe it's something else. Your school nurse or family doctor will be able to make suggestions on how to help you so you don't feel so tired.

q: There's a freak at my school who dresses like a witch, and I hate her. My friends make fun of her, but the little freak still dresses like a witch. Does she worship Satan or what?

a: I have no idea who she worships, and that's really a stupid question. The question you should be asking yourself is: Why does it matter how this girl dresses?

You, girl, are worrying *way* too much about someone else when you should be paying attention to yourself.

You want to know the truth? This girl is in her power because she's dressing the way she wants to dress. You, though, are losing your power because you're spending so much time worrying about someone else.

It sounds like the reason you're freaking out is because you don't know how to deal with someone who's different from you.

To you, it's really important to fit in. But for this girl, that isn't important. She likes to express herself through her clothing. What's wrong with that? Absolutely nothing!

Say you and your friends all dress in blue. That's fine. You all look the same and none of you feel different.

But what if a rainbow only had one color?

It wouldn't be a rainbow, would it? It would just be a blue streak. A blue streak might be pretty to look at, but it certainly isn't as beautiful as a rainbow!

Now let's say this girl you don't like dresses in orange.

Who's to say that orange isn't as pretty as blue? Or that red isn't prettier than both of them! My point is, it takes a bunch of different colors to make a rainbow!

Rather than act cruelly toward this girl, why don't you try to understand that there are going to be many people in this world who are different from you? Rather than hate this girl—which sounds like it's hurting you more than her—why not appreciate the fact that she's bringing a whole new color to the rainbow?

Who knows? By doing this, maybe you'll discover that your world has become a little more beautiful.

q: I'm thinking about getting my nose pierced, and I really want a tattoo. But my ogre mother says I can't get either until I'm eighteen. Why do parents have to be so lame?

a: To tell you the truth, your parents aren't being lame. They're just concerned about you.

See, the reason parents tell us we have to wait until we're eighteen before we do the big stuff is 'cause we live in their houses. And we'll probably be living there until we're eighteen!

Seriously, the reason your parents seem strict is that they realize you're getting more mature—but it's a process that has only just started. You're on your way to becoming an adult, but you're not an adult yet.

That's not to say you'll totally be an adult at eighteen. But at least your brain will be more developed, and you'll have more experience making decisions for yourself.

And that's really the bottom line. Your parents

don't want you to make a mistake you might regret.

Besides, here's something very important to consider about tattoos: They're almost absolutely permanent. Sure, you can undergo a painful procedure involving a laser to remove a tattoo. What happens is, most of the tattoo (but not all) gets burned off your skin. Can we say "major pain"?

I personally believe there are very creative ways to decorate your body that don't involve pain and are not permanent. Temporary tattoos, cool nail polish, funky clothes, wild hair color, etc.

Try to look for a unique way to express yourself. Something that's not painful—and definitely not permanent!

q: I recently read that Fiona Apple is a vegetarian. I've decided to try and become one too. Why do most people become vegetarians anyway?

a: Some people are turning to a vegetarian way of eating, which means they no longer eat meat or products containing meat.

Most girls who choose not to eat meat do this because the thought of eating a cuddly cow or a cute little pig really grosses them out or makes them feel sad. While I applaud their sensitivity, I also have to encourage every girl thinking about becoming a vegetarian to discuss this matter with a doctor, a nutritionist, or a school nurse.

See, our bodies are going through a lot of changes right now, and we absolutely need certain things—vitamins, minerals, proteins, and carbohydrates—to grow properly. And the best way to get these things if from the foods we eat. But there's no single food that can provide you with everything your body needs to grow properly. So you have to eat a bunch of different foods.

If you take meat out of your diet, you need to get all the important stuff you normally get from meat—like protein—from other foods.

I'm not saying you should not become vegetarian. But I definitely think you should check with your family doctor or a school nurse before you change the way you eat.

q: I want braces but my family can't afford them. Is there a cheap way to get them? I want a silvery smile!

a: I feel for you because it's hard to want something and not be able to get it! And if your family doesn't have dental insurance (or the extra cash lying around), it can be impossible to even think about getting braces because they're so expensive.

That said, I have something to share that hopefully will help you feel a little better. My parents recently took me to an orthodontist, who said I needed braces to correct a slight overbite.

After considering my options for a few days, I decided *not* to get the braces. The reason? Well, you don't have to look any further than Tom Cruise's goofy grin, Jewel's protruding tooth, or the gap between Madonna's teeth.

Tom, Jewel, and Madonna have nice teeth—but their teeth are not perfect! They have what my mom calls "character." It's interesting to look at these superstars because they *aren't* perfect.

Now, I'm not saying you don't need braces. Only an orthodontist can tell you that. But if your family can't afford braces—don't feel bad. You might have a very pretty smile and not even realize it yet!

Just remember to take good care of your teeth by brushing and flossing. A healthy and natural smile—even if it's not a silvery one—is very pretty.

q: There's this girl on my bus who calls me Pelican. At first I didn't know why—until I saw a pelican. She was making fun of my nose! I wanted to beat her up after that. So one day I pushed her. She started crying like I'd just beat the crap out of her, and she turned me in to the principal. I got so busted. But my question is, I've seen guys do a lot worse—like actually punch another guy. And they totally don't get into trouble. It's like teachers don't care if a guy gets into a fight. But if a girl even tries to start a fight, she practically gets arrested! What's up with that?

a: Well, my own personal feeling is that any time someone becomes aggressive with another person, they should get busted. Physical violence (and even if you only pushed her, you were still violent) is so stupid. It's like, *hello!* How would you feel if someone came up and pushed you? You'd be scared, right? And who wants to go to school and feel scared?

As for boys punching each other and not getting busted, I think some unfortunate teachers and principals think it's macho for guys to fight. Like it's expected of them or something. That's just stupid. I do know some bully guys, but I'm not friends with them because they're jerks. My friends who are guys don't want to be hit any more than they want to hit someone else.

This whole physical violence thing is just ridiculous.

But even though I think physical violence is stupid, I don't necessarily think being angry with another person is stupid. It's perfectly natural to feel anger toward people. I personally feel angry whenever I see someone treating another person badly.

But do I go over and beat that person up? No. Do I go over and say, "You're a total jerk for being mean to that person"? No. I can't control what other kids do to each other, much as I'd like to try!

So what do I do? Well, I don't let the anger simmer inside me, that's for sure. I get my anger out. Not with flying fists, but with flying fingers!

I write in my journal. Sometimes just seeing how angry I feel on paper helps me feel better. It's like punching something without being stupid enough to actually hit it.

I've realized I can take out all my anger (yes, girls do feel very angry sometimes) on paper.

And when I want to get really violent (on paper, of course!), I write in red ink. I know it sounds kind of morbid, but red is the color of anger.

Writing in red ink helps me feel mad without doing anything stupid.

Another great way I work through my anger is by getting physical. I jump rope. Or I take a bike ride. Or anything else I can think of to help me chill out.

I just realized, and you should realize too, that it's better to get your anger out than to hold it in. Sure, it's stupid to get into a physical fight. But that doesn't mean I can't be angry in other ways.

But I get angry without getting into trouble. Maybe you should try it too.

q: There is this guy who gets off at my bus stop and always makes remarks about my boobs. I'm pretty developed compared to other girls, and this creep is bringing all this unwanted attention to me. Can you tell me what to do, please?!!

a: This is a really complex question. It's complex because this boy is making you feel bad about yourself. You're becoming embarrassed and maybe even a little ashamed.

What this boy is doing is *wrong*. You have to understand that this guy is *harassing* you. He is picking on you because of something that make you a girl—the fact that you have breasts. Because he's making you feel uncomfortable with your breasts, he's *sexually* harassing you.

He needs to be taught, right now, that girls are not to be sexually harassed.

Here's what you do. The next time this boy makes a comment about your breasts, say very firmly and clearly, "I'm telling you to leave me alone. If you do not stop, I am reporting the harassment." He might laugh and not take you seriously.

The next time he does it, go immediately to the principal of your school and report exactly what the boy is doing or saying. Tell your parents as well. Everyone needs to know about this situation.

Sexual harassment by boys is never to be tolerated. *Ever.*

Your body is very powerful. Never let him or anyone else make you feel ashamed or embarrassed because of your power.

q: I love music. The more depressing the better. Most girls my age like such stupid music! There's nothing I like more than turning off the lights in my room, lighting a candle and incense, and just getting lost in the music. Is this normal?

a: I, too, like turning to music to zone out and be alone. Music is a very important part of my life. Sometimes, if I am feeling lonely or sad or bored, just hearing a song that expresses the way I feel makes me feel better.

What worries me is that you say, "The more depressing the better." Does that mean you like to be depressed? Or do you just like dark, moody music?

Hopefully, it just means you like music that makes you think and feel in new and different ways.

There's something important to remember about music and the lyrics to songs. Whoever wrote the song is only expressing the way they felt at that moment. And when you listen to the song, you might feel that way too.

But the person who wrote the song doesn't feel that way *all* the time. And you should pay close attention to how the song encourages you to feel.

If it encourages you to feel sad or bad in any way for a long time, you should choose more uplifting music.

Music doesn't have to be peppy to be cool. But if the music you're listening to is making you depressed, you should definitely turn it off. Then do some writing in your journal to figure out why you're feeling the way you are.

q: Camy, I noticed in your previous books that your publisher is in New York. My goal is to be on MTV, and I know MTV's offices are in New York too. Do you know anyone at MTV who you can introduce me to? I'm willing to pay you. I'm thirteen and I really, really want to be a VJ! By the way, do you ever run into any VJ's in New York? If you do, tell them about me! Maybe we could all get together for lunch—my treat!

a: I get some funny mail, dear readers, but this one takes the cake!

For the record, my publisher is in New York, but I am not. *Hello!* I live in Peoria. And I don't know anyone at MTV. Though I would love to meet a particular VJ (cute guy with brown hair, totally great personality!), I'm not going to embarrass myself by naming him!

By the way, I think you have to be at least eighteen to be a VJ! Sorry!

final words

until we meet again!

as usual, I had so much fun writing this book, I wish it didn't have to end! But alas, my dear readers, I must return to my schoolwork! Yikes!

Before I go, I'd like to take this time to thank you. Not only because you bought this book—although I *really* appreciate that!—but also because you've helped me learn so much about myself.

Let me explain.

You might think I know all the answers to everything 'cause my books are so fun and informative! (At least you *better* think that!☺)

Well, the truth is: I'm just as confused about

165

things as you are. It takes a lot of effort on my part to really figure things out and try to make sense of them in my books.

With your support, though, I've had the opportunity to learn *many* new things. So, in a way, writing for you helps me a lot too. *That's* why I thank you.

Okay, with that out of the way, here's a reminder: Visit my Web site at www.camybaker. com! By the way, if you or your school doesn't have access to the Internet, your local library should. All you have to do is tell the librarian you want to do some Web surfing, and they should be able to help you. ☺

This is Camy Baker, signing off with wishes for peace and love!

LYLAS,
Camy Baker

reference

rules at a glance

for easy reference

1. Accept your body exactly the way it is.

2. Realize you're more than a reflection.

3. Limit your time in front of the mirror.

4. Reprogram your thoughts.

5. Water—you need water!

6. Fuel your body.

7. Listen to your body.

8. Stop pinching yourself!

9. Go for strength, not thinness.

10. Keep yourself well groomed.

11. Ready or not—here it comes.

12. It's your puberty and you can cry if you want to.

13. Relax, it's just your hormones.

14. Get physical.

15. Stay true to yourself.

16. Don't be a TV clone.

17. Become *super*aware of commercials.

18. Try not to take fashion mags too seriously.

19. It's okay if you don't look like a model.

20. Choose to be beautiful.

21. Stay out of the beauty war.

22. Look good for you, not boys.

23. Protect your power.

24. Communicate with your parents.

25. Help your sister.

26. Be creative.

27. Give every class your best effort.

28. Look for positive role models.

29. Discover new interests.

30. Never let your power go.

and finally, check out

web site
www.camybaker.com

see ya there!!!

bye!